Eamonn,

thank you for
making my life a
little less painful.

Happy
reading

E. W. Richardson

The Urchin Warriors

of Love and War

By

R. W. Nichelson

"Based on Actual Events"

This book is dedicated to the men on both sides of the conflict who, at one time, were mortal enemies and through the passing of time became both allies and brothers. And to those brave men who made the ultimate sacrifice, deserving to never be forgotten.

Introduction

Kristian Ackmann, is a young German soldier in the elite 12th SS Hitler youth Panzer division. He is given the assignment of defending Caen in France near the Normandy coast, against the inevitable allied invasion. On his way he meets Holly Petit, a beautiful and inviting young French girl. They unexpectedly fall madly and passionately in love amid the chaos, and horrors of war. The romance these two young lovers share, must be hidden so that Holly humiliating torment by her countrymen. This as well as being shunned, or worse, for collaborating with the enemy. The book is an exciting and action-packed story of intrigue, forbidden love, and the discovery of faith. In the middle of the greatest war, the world has ever known.

Love can't conquer war, but can it survive one?

Chapter One

Kristian was in horrified shock at what he was seeing; something worse than any nightmare he could possibly ever imagine. As he knelt on the floor holding his dying mothers' hand, Kristian looked into her eyes and watched as her blood and life slowly drained from her body. Both his mothers' legs, one of her arms, and most of her flesh was ripped from her loving face. Her body, burn near to a crisp by the bombs being dropped by the British aircraft. From that moment on, Kristian vowed to devote his entire existence to the revenge of his mother's death. Kristian was determined the English would pay dearly for what they had done to him, and all of those he knew and loved.

April 20th, 1944, was Hitler's 55th birthday, and just a year before the Fuhrer's death and the total destruction of his Thousand-Year Reich. April 20th also happened to be Kristian Ackmann's, of the 12th SS Panzer HJ Division's, 18th birthday. Kristian had the honor of sharing his birthday with his Fuhrer, but to his misfortune had to celebrate this momentous occasion in a rocky foxhole on the perimeter around an airfield near Dreux France, a town just short of 200 kilometers (124 miles) east of Caen.

Kristian was day-dreaming thinking of all the little things he could be doing with Holly right now. Holly was a young French girl who had captured Kristian's heart and as with young love, she was all Kristian could think about. Rudy, a ginger-haired 17-year-old boy from Dresden, ran up to Kristian's foxhole. Rudy was a runner for Kristian's division, delivering messages from headquarters to the troops on the line. "Kristian," Rudy said, panting from his repeated sprint from foxhole to foxhole.

"Hey, Rudy," Kristian said. "What's going on?"

"Tomorrow we are to start training for the invasion of Europe by the Allies. Rumor has it that they're planning to invade under the command of General Patton," Rudy explained.

"Patton, he is a tough general, that doesn't sound good. Any idea where they might land on the coast?" Kristian said.

"They think it'll either happen at the Pas-de-Calais or Normandy, but most likely the Pas-de-Calais," Rudy said.

"God, I hope it is there and not here," Kristian said, not wanting to take on the British and Americans as well as the Russians.

"Good luck my friend," Rudy told Kristian with a small smile and a look of sincere concern in his eyes then quickly ran off to the next foxhole.

A sense of dread came over Kristian. Everyone knew that Germany was losing the war, and that soon all this madness would finally end. Even though many of his comrades were fanatical Nazis, no one wanted to be the last man to die in a

3

winless war. Otto Kruger, a young man from Frankfurt who was the perfect example of a man of Hitler's Aryan master race with his blond hair and piercing blue eyes, was sharing the foxhole with Kristian.

"Don't worry," Otto told Kristian. "Everything will be just fine. Hey, that's pretty neat that your birthday is the same as our Fuhrer's is."

"Yeah," Kristian said with a small chuckle. "I remember when I was a small boy my mother bought a birthday cake for me and it had a picture of the Fuhrer on it made of icing. It really upset me, and I started crying. My mother asked me what was wrong and I told her that the cake was for Hitler's birthday, not mine, and that I wanted a birthday cake for me. My mother realized how upset I was because my birthday was overshadowed by the Fuhrer's. She gave me a hug, then told me that only a few people share something that special with our Fuhrer and it was something she said that I should be proud of. Of course, not knowing any better, that cheered me up and gave me a whole new outlook. It made me feel like I had a special connection with

4

the Fuhrer. It's funny how a young mind thinks," Kristian said with a snicker.

He thought back to those younger years, and the connection that he not only felt with the Fuhrer for sharing the same birthday but to the Reich itself. It was as if they were growing and aging together. Kristian knew it was coming to an end, the death of the Reich. *Would it be his demise as well?* he wondered to himself. *How could the master race be defeated by subhuman cultures,* Kristian pondered? Was everything they were taught, a lie?

Education in the German Third Reich indoctrinated students with the National Socialist view of the world. Nazi educators glorified the Nordic and other "Aryan" races, while degrading Jews and other so-called inferior people as parasites or "bastard races" incapable of creating a civilized culture. Kristian joined the HJ (Hitler Jugend or Hitler Youth) at the age of ten in 1936, when membership in Nazi youth groups became mandatory for all boys and girls between the ages of ten and seventeen. After school, Kristian and the other children would have meetings and weekend camping trips sponsored by the government of the Third Reich. The Hitler Youth (HJ) and the League of German Girls trained children like Kristian to become faithful to the Nazi Party and Germany's Thousand-Year Reich.

Kristian trained in a combination of sports, artistic education, physical fitness and Nazi ideology. Similarly, the League of German Girls emphasized athletics, such as rhythmic gymnastics, which the Nazi party deemed less strenuous to the female body and better geared to preparing them for motherhood. These values encouraged young men and women to abandon their individuality in favor of the goals of the new Aryan ideology. Kristian and other boys from age ten to fourteen belonged to the *Deutshes Jungvolk*, (German Youth) and from the ages fourteen to eighteen Kristian was in the actual HJ. Each boy was also given a performance booklet detailing his progress in athletics and Nazi indoctrination throughout the time spent in the HJ.

Within the HJ was the *Streifendienst* (Patrol Force), they functioned as internal political police. Their assignment was to sustain order at meetings, weeding out disloyal members, and denouncing anyone who criticized Hitler or Nazism including, in some cases, their own parents. One case involved a young teenager named Walter Hess who turned his father into the Gestapo for calling Hitler a crazed maniac. Walter's father was quickly hauled off to the Dachau concentration camp in what the Reich called *Schutzhaft* (protective custody). For the boy setting such a good example to his peers, Walter was promoted to a higher rank within the HJ to motivate others in devotion to the Reich.

Through the years of war, Kristian saw fathers and older brothers killed in battle, their cities bombed to oblivion. Innocent women and children killed with indiscretion that hardened the young man and gave him a burning hatred of the allies, due to what he saw as their heartless aggression. The indoctrination of Nazi ideology and the horrors he was experiencing at the hands of the enemy, gave Kristian a fanatical desire to fight and, if necessary, gladly die for his Fuhrer and Fatherland.

By 1943, with the loss of 91,000 soldiers at the battle of Stalingrad, Germany began to become desperate for men to serve as combat troops. The HJ transitioned itself from a Boy Scout-type of program to a more militaristic training mission teaching

7

skills such as marksmanship and military tactics. This would give Kristian a good foundation and a head start in the transition to military life.

With the ever-increasing losses of men on the Eastern front, the German high command concluded that Germany had to declare, "Total War," and this could only be brought about by uncommon efforts. The formation of an SS division utilizing the boys in the HJ was a big part of this new program to turn the tide of the war.

In November of 1943, at the age of 17, Kristian was recruited into the HJ Division of the 12th SS and began the SS training program. He was ordered to report to Unna Railway Station and there, board a train that would take him and other young men to the training center. At the station were hundreds of boys and here Kristian met Otto. He noticed a blond-haired boy standing nearby holding the same type of Persil (soap powder box or a small suitcase) in his hand, and decided to walk over and chat with the boy.

"Hey," Kristian said loudly so to be heard over all of the other boys talking and horseplay. "We have the exact same suitcase," The boy looked down at Kristian's suitcase and back at his face and smiled without saying a word. Kristian stuck out his hand and said. "Hi, I'm Kristian, what's your name?"

"Otto," the boy said and happily shook Kristian's hand.

"This is pretty exciting isn't it?" Kristian said with a look of enthusiasm on his face.

"Yes, it is."

"I've always wanted to join the SS."

"Me too". "My father was in the Waffen SS. He was killed on the Russian front last year"

"Oh, I'm sorry to hear that, Kristian said with a look of sympathy on his face. I lost an uncle in Poland back in 1939. I didn't know him too well, and I know it's not as bad as losing your dad but I think just about everyone has lost someone in their family in the war." Otto gave Kristian a small crooked smile and shook his head in agreement.

A conductor yelled and ordered them to board the train. No one was sure of their destination, it was quite the mystery, and the boys threw out guesses to each other on where they might be going. Kristian and Otto sat together in the rail car so they would have some familiar company for the journey to their destination. The need for each other would soon be more desperate than just the need for each other's company.

The sun had gone down, and most of the boys were tired from the excitement of anticipation. The train slowly pulled away from the station and the rail car became quiet. The boys would soon succumb to the need for slumber by the repetitive sound of the train rolling along the rails of the track. It was an opportunity that they surely needed to take advantage of.

After passing the German-Belgian town of Turnhout the boys arrived at their destination station. The recruits were put in formation and marched to the quarters of the *Aufklurungsabteilung* (reconnaissance unit) that was just being set up. Otto leaned over to Kristian and said quietly, "I wonder what this place is?"

"I don't know, Kristian said. "But it looks like we are about to find out; there's a *Standartenfuhrer* (Colonel) walking this way."

"*Achtung*," yelled the sergeant in charge of the formation. All of the new recruits snapped to attention in unison.

The Colonel stood in front of the formation. "You young men have been selected to form a new regiment called the 12th SS HJ Division. You'll be divided up in groups according to the unit you'll be assigned to, and you'll then be sent to your respective training areas.

"I know you men will gladly make the ultimate sacrifice for your Fuhrer and Fatherland if necessary. Remember our motto, 'Live Faithfully, Fight Bravely, and Die Laughing.' We were born to die for Germany. You are nothing–your *Volk* (People) is everything." The Colonel then raised his arm in a Nazi salute and bellowed "Heil Hitler." In unison, the recruits snapped their heels together and returned the salute to the Colonel. "Heil Hitler." "I guess we now know," Kristian said quietly to Otto. Otto just looked at Kristian with an acknowledging cat ate the canary grin.

Chapter Two

Two NCO's divided the boys into groups of about 75 men each. Then all hell broke loose. "You dirty maggots," The NCO's shouted, and those were the nicer words they used. "Get down and low crawl pushing your suitcases in front of you through the gate," All the boys dropped to the ground. Kristian and Otto looked at each other wide eyed with fear on their faces. "Move, move, move you little bastards," The NCO's bellowed to the boys.

After all of the boys had made it past the gate, the NCO's allowed them to stand and then were ran to their assigned barracks. Once all the boys were squared away and assigned bunks, they were ordered to stand at attention at the end of their bunks. It was now 4 p.m. and the boys were starving. One of the boys said, "when do we get to eat?" The entire group would soon be sorry he had said that question, As the boys immediately began learning the more eloquent words the drill sergeants knew. It was 8 p.m. that night when the boys finally received their meager first meal. After that the boys were allowed to go to bed. That was day one.

At 6 a.m. the next morning the drill instructors woke the new recruits using whistles and the sound of metal trash cans being kicked across the barracks floor, along with the screaming of every profane word they could pull from their sadistic minds. Most of the boys were so shocked they almost fell out of bed, including Kristian and Otto.

"Son of a bitch, what the hell is going on?" Otto said completely bewildered.

"I don't know but it can't be good," Kristian said just as confused.

"Welcome to day two ladies," one drill instructor yelled.

There was no chow hall, so two boys were selected to go get coffee and the morning ration of bread and jelly and bring it back to the barracks. "You two," one of the drill instructors bellowed pointing at Kristian and Otto. "Run directly across the compound and get this morning's rations."

"Yes sergeant," both boys yelled out, then sprinted out of the barracks as fast as their feet could carry them. "Damn, I'm glad to get out of there," Kristian said to Otto as they ran across the compound.

"Me too, I don't think those guys like us," Otto said sarcastically, laughing as they ran.

Kristian and Otto reached the building where the recruits chow was prepared and quickly ran inside the front door. There were several other boys standing in line to receive the morning rations for their assigned groups. Kristian and Otto fell in line behind the last man. The line moved rather quickly and the boys reached the distribution point. Kristian noticed a strange but at the same time familiar smell.

"What's that smell?" Kristian said the SS *oberschutze* (private first class) handing out the rations with a hint of a stink face.

"That would be the coffee," the private answered. Kristian looked into the large vat that was on the table in front of him filled with the pungent liquid.

"That's black and it looks hot, but that definitely isn't coffee," he said to the private.

"That's the closest you're going to get to it here so be happy to get it. Now, get your rations and move on; I have a lot of people to feed."

The boys grabbed their allotted rations and headed back to their barracks straining from the load that they were carrying. "Boy, I hope we don't have to do this every day," Otto said with a grunt as he walked.

"If it gets us away from that mean-ass drill instructor I don't mind at all," Kristian said, eyes wide open with a chuckle and a smile. Otto returned the smile and the chuckle, shaking his head with agreement as the boys carried on with their struggle across the compound.

After the young recruits finished their morning cuisine, they were ordered out to a formation in front of the barracks, then marched over to the supply building to be issued their new uniforms. All the boys fell out with excitement to get their uniforms and gear. The new recruits were not trusted with a rifle yet, that would come later. "I can't wait to get my uniform," Otto said, almost giddy with excitement. Kristian shook his head and rolled his eyes.

"Calm down; before it's all over, you'll probably be sick of that uniform."

The boys began being issued their uniforms. There were three complete uniforms: camouflage field dress, a grey standard uniform and, everyone's favorite, the black Panzer uniform. "Do not touch the black," It is to go in your locker, the drill sergeant shouted over the boys chattering. I don't want you idiots screwing up your uniforms." The boys all groaned with disappointment and became silent through the rest of the issuing process.

Once the issuing of uniforms was complete, the young recruits were marched back to their barracks and spent the rest of

16

the day being instructed on how to store their equipment and uniforms. Everything had to be sparkling clean, and in their proper places at all times. Failure to do this would lead to severe punishment, which every recruit wanted to avoid. "Listen up, ladies," the drill instructor yelled. "The rest of the day is yours. Fall in at 06:00 in the morning in your grey uniform, and I better be able to see my reflection in the shine of your boots."

"I guess I know what we'll be doing the rest of the night," Otto said with raised brow. "We're going to be polishing our boots."

"No doubt about that," Kristian said. "Hey, let's check the board before we get started and see what we're doing tomorrow." The boys ran over to the bulletin board to see what the day would bring, with excitement and smiles on their faces. Reading the board, Kristian said, "Tomorrow is marching and close-order drill."

The boys looked at each other. The excited smiles on their faces quickly faded away and they slowly walked back to their bunks, their heads held low in disappointment. "I wanted to get our rifles and go shooting at the range," Otto mumbled to himself.

"Don't worry," Kristian said. "I'm sure we will get them soon enough; it's going to be our job so I would imagine we will get plenty of chance to shoot. Let's get our boots polished so we don't get our butts kicked in the morning,"

The next morning Kristian and Otto found out that they had two left feet and two left hands, and that they couldn't do anything right in the eyes of their drill instructors. The instructors were constantly yelling at the new recruits. They never realized that a German could be the lowest form on earth and were told in terms they could not imagine. The gentler insults were *Scheisskopf* (shithead) and *Arschloch* (assholes); the others were more severe.

Around noon the recruits were allowed lunch. This consisted of bean soup, three boiled potatoes served in a metal bowl, and *kommissbrot* (a piece of bread). Since there was not a mess hall the boys had to find a place where they could eat. A bowl of soup, three potatoes and a piece of bread was a little hard to handle with just two hands. If the recruits dropped anything, which was easy to do, the lovely drill sergeant was right there in your face to encourage you to hold them correctly without dropping anything.

One of the new recruits had the misfortune of making this mistake and immediately regretted it. "You don't want your food, precious?" the instructor yelled at the boy. "It's not good enough for your discerning pallet? Get your dumb ass up and dump the rest of your food next to that mess. You get down and eat it like the pig you are or go hungry until the night meal." Needless to say, none of the recruits dropped their food for the rest of the training program.

The recruits were allowed one-hour lunch, and in the afternoon, there were classes about weapons, tactics, and of course, Nazi doctrine. At 6 p.m. the day was over as far as classes were concerned and the boys had free time until 10 p.m. when it was lights out.

"Hey Krissy, check the bulletin board to see what we are doing tomorrow," Otto told Kristian.

"Okay," Kristian said, "Looks like we're to be issued rifles and go to the field for tactics training.

"Fantastic," Otto said, smiling ear-to-ear.

"We're finally getting our weapons; I can't wait."

One of the drill instructors entered the barracks door and yelled inside, "Listen up you idiots, make sure you are in formation at 06:00 in the morning. Camouflage uniforms and tactical gear. Make sure your gear is squared away. You're going to need it." The room was silent. The boys were all looking at each other in disbelief at the wonderful news they were hearing.

"Did you idiots hear me?" the drill instructor yelled.

"Yes, drill instructor," all the boys said in unison. "Finally," Otto said to Kristian. "We're going to get to do the fun stuff,"

"I know," Kristian said just as excited about the news, isn't it great? We better get our shit together and ready for tomorrow." The boys spent the rest of the evening making sure their gear was ready in excited anticipation of the coming day. "We better get some rest tonight; I bet they have us running our asses off tomorrow," Kristian said to Otto, but because of their excitement they were going to find it a sleepless night.

Kristian and Otto entered the barracks the following day exhausted and dirty from the days training. The task of the day had been to familiarize themselves with the pincer movement, or the double envelopment of an enemy force. This is a military maneuver in which units simultaneously attack both flanks (sides) of an enemy. The name comes from visualizing the action as the divided attacking forces "pinching" the enemy. This maneuver can have excellent results in capturing many of the enemy's forces and large areas of enemy occupied territory.

The boys were bunked side by side, and they both immediately flopped on their bunks with what they felt was the last bit of energy they could muster. Their limp, dirty, sweaty bodies spread out across their beds, eyes staring at the ceiling in undying gratitude to God for the day to be finally over. "Do you think every day will be like this?" Otto said without moving a muscle still staring at the ceiling.

"Lord I hope not, I don't think it could get much worse than it was today," Kristian said. Little did they both know that soon they would look back at this as the good old days.

"I'm starving," Otto moaned as he put his hand on his stomach. "We haven't eaten since yesterday. It feels like one side of my stomach is trying to eat the other."

"I know," Kristian said. "Let's get cleaned up and get us something to eat."

"You don't have to tell me twice," Otto said as he sprung to his feet and began to remove his gear. I'm going to get me a full belly and sleep for two days."

"I don't think that is going to happen," Kristian said to Otto.

"Why is that?" Otto said.

"I saw the roster on the wall on the way in. We both have guard duty at 6 a.m.," Kristian said.

"Oh crap," was all Otto could say as he lowered his shoulders and dropped his head, surrendering to his doom.

"It'll be okay, buddy," Kristian said.

"All we have to do is stand around and talk all day; it'll be a breeze. Now let's get us a shower and something to eat."

The boys stripped down to their skivvies and headed to the shower. They stood next to each other and turned on the refreshing warm water, letting the water pour over their tired, dirty bodies. Otto noticed Kristian chuckling to himself. "What's so funny?" Otto said. "I see your mother didn't give you any toys to play with," Kristian said, snickering.

"Hey, screw you. And keep your eyes to yourself, pervert," Otto said angrily

"Don't worry buddy; I won't tell anyone if it was an inch shorter you would be a girl. Now I understand why you're so sensitive." Otto gave Kristian a not so subtle hand sign of just what he thought of Kristian's ribbing, then refused to talk to Kristian the rest of the evening.

Chapter Three

Later in the training the boys of the 12th SS were

dispersed and billeted in local families' houses, schools or halls.

There was little free time for the recruits, but the time they did

have, they were encouraged to get to know their hosts. Kristian

and the other boys were to learn their life styles and way of

thinking in order to build a stronger relationship between them

and The Reich.

One afternoon after a light day of training, Kristian

strolled along the streets of Leopoldsburg just to get a feel of the

town and enjoy a little quiet time all to himself. (This was an

opportunity that was rare, and he had to take advantage of it

while he could). Leopoldsburg is a small town located in the

Belgian province of Limburg, a town Kristian would never forget. Holly Petit, just as her name, was a petite girl with long brown hair and smooth, dusky skin. Holly had big brown eyes surrounded by pearl white sclera.

Holly spotted Kristian walking down the empty sidewalk staring at the ground as if deep in thought. Intrigued by this tall young stranger, she decided to discreetly attract his attention. Coming toward Kristian, Holly intentionally bumped into Kristian with her shoulder as she hurriedly passed by him, as if late for an important affair.

"Excuse me," Holly said, as if annoyed by Kristian's carelessness. "Do you always assault young ladies in the street?"

Kristian looked up from the ground at Holly, a slightly shocked and penitent expression on his face. Kristian immediately noticed Holly's natural beauty. Kristian also noticed there was absolutely no one else on the street, just the two of them. e knew the game the young woman was playing and decided to play along.

"Uh no, I mean, I'm sorry miss; I didn't see you," Kristian said, trying to hold back a smile his face was determined to display.

"Is that how the German Army teaches their soldiers to treat defenseless women?" Holly said with a slight growl.

"No miss, it's not, and I apologize," Kristian said. "And I'm in the SS, not the army."

"That's even worse," Holly fired back at Kristian. "I know all about you SS. You're all evil and rotten to the core," glaring back at Kristian with a look of utter disgust on her face.

"Were not all bad," Kristian tried to explain. "I'm a nice guy, really. Just give me a chance, let me make it up to you. Let me buy you a cup of coffee. It'll give you a chance to get to know me a little better and you'll see. I'm really not that bad. What do you say? Give me a chance," Kristian said with the most piteous expression he could muster.

"Well, okay," Holly said empathetically. "Everyone deserves a chance."

"Wonderful, thank you," Kristian said with a smile of gratitude.

"Do you know where we could get some coffee? I'm kind of new to this town and don't know my way around very well."

"Yes," Holly said. "There's a nice café just around the corner. Come with me."

Kristian and Holly began their walk to the café and carried on with the conversation along the way. "The coffee is not that great due to rationing, but it's the best you can get around here," Holly explained.

"That's okay, I'm used to bad coffee," Kristian said with a smile. "What is your name?"

"I'm Holly, Holly Petit," she said.

"Well that's fitting," Kristian said with a slightly mischievous smile. "My name is Kristian, nice to meet you Holly," Kristian said with a grin as he offered his hand to shake hers.

"Holly?" Kristian said with a puzzled look on his face. "That's British, isn't it?"

"My grandfather fought in World War I, he came from England and while he was here found himself a war bride and married my grandmother. They had my mother and she married my father, a Dutchman and had me. My parents named me after my grandfather's mother, Holly, and that's how I got my name." They both looked at each other with a humored smile and continued their leisurely stroll to the café.

The young couple entered the café and sat down at a table, then ordered their coffee. "You know it's not proper for a French girl to fraternize with a German; I worry what people might think," Holly said quietly to Kristian, as she looked around the room to see if anyone was watching them.

"Don't worry Holly. No one is going to say anything while I'm around," he said proudly.

"It's what they might do after you leave is what worries me," Holly said with a whisper and a slight look of fear.

"Don't worry, everything will be fine," Kristian said trying to reassure Holly. "Tell me, where are you from?" Kristian said in an attempt to quickly change the subject and get Holly's mind off her fear.

"Originally, I'm from here but my family moved to Caen in France when I was a young girl; it's my home now. It's where I grew up. How about you? Where do you call home?"

"I don't have one," Kristian said. "My home was destroyed in a British bombing raid one night. I guess this is home now," he said holding up both hands and a shrug of his shoulders.

"I'm sorry to hear that Kristian," Holly said with a sincere look of empathy. "It must be hard. Do you have family back in Germany?"

"No," Kristian said. "My father and uncle died on the Eastern Front and my mother and sister in the bombing raid. That's all the family I had. I guess I'm an orphan now," he said in an attempt to lighten the conversation a bit.

"You poor thing," Holly said with a look on her face as if she were about to cry. "No wonder you're a misguided little Nazi, you have no one to teach you any better."

"I'm not a misguided little Nazi. I know exactly what I'm doing," Kristian said with just a hint of frustration. "The Fuhrer is trying to make this a better world, and the Jews, the communists and imperialists are trying to destroy Germany because of it. Those greedy criminals want to enslave the German people and our Fuhrer is the only thing that is keeping them from doing it. Things are looking a little bad for the Reich right now, but the Fuhrer says we have wonder weapons that soon will be operational and with them we shall win the war. The Third Reich will then take its rightful place as the leader in a new world order."

"Oh honey, you are so misguided and brainwashed you can't even see the truth," Holly said, concerned for Kristian.

"The truth," Kristian said. "The truth is the Fuhrer saved Germany from its demise and made it great again. The truth is the Allies bomb our cities day and night killing thousands of innocent men, women and children with careless abandon. They don't give a damn about the horror they put our people through. People who are harmless and have done absolutely nothing to no one. No Holly, I'm hardly misguided."

Clearly angry about the conversation, Kristian quickly stood up out of his chair and began to leave the café.

"Wait Kristian, don't go. I'm sorry," Holly said as she stood up and reached across the table to grasp Kristian's hand. "I didn't realize how much you hurt," Holly said with remorse for bringing such anguish to Kristian. "Please stay. We will talk of something else. Something other than this damn war. Please Kristian."

31

Kristian looked at Holly and saw the sincerity in her face. "I'm sorry Holly," Kristian said as they both sat back down, still holding each other's hand. "I shouldn't let things get to me like that."

For the rest of the afternoon the young couple sat in the café talking, getting to know everything they could about each other. The hours passed by and rarely did either let go of the other's hand the entire evening. They had just met but they both knew that this was love. From different countries, on opposite sides of the war and with completely opposed ideologies they shared one thing, a passionate burning desire for one another. Together they had created a flame that would never be extinguished, a fire so strong, not even war could put out.

It was getting late and Kristian had to report back to the house where he was billeted before he was put on report for not being at his duty station. Kristian walked Holly to her uncle's house where her family was staying during their visit, continuing to talk and learning all they could of each other's life. About a block away from Holly's uncle's home Holly stopped.

"Kristian," Holly said. "Please don't come any further. I don't want my family to see me with you. They would go insane if they saw me with you and they would never allow me to see you again. Give me some time to figure out how to tell them about you, please."

"Okay Holly," Kristian said. "I understand. When can I see you again?"

"My parents and my uncle and aunt are going to Brussels this weekend. Can you come see me Saturday?" Holly said with anticipation.

"I'll try, I promise," Kristian said. "If I'm not here by noon I can't make it, but I'll do everything I can to be here."

Holly gave Kristian a huge smile then stood up on the tips of her toes and gave Kristian a quick kiss on the cheek. He stood and watched with a smile as Holly ran toward her uncle's house with a smile enjoying every flowing movement Holly made on her way. Just before reaching the house, Holly quickly turned around as she ran, giving Kristian one last smile and wave before going into the house. Kristian returned both smile and wave and watched the beautiful young woman he had just lost his heart to close the door behind her.

Kristian slowly walked back to where he was billeted thinking of Holly and the lovely afternoon he had spent with her. Holly magically made him feel as he had never felt before. It was a mixture of inner peace, joy, confusion and a new strange feeling of loneliness without her presence. Kristian's concerns were only thought of day by day. Now, somehow, his meeting with Holly gave him a whole new outlook, thoughts of the future and how things might be. How pleasant it would be to spend the rest of his days with Holly and the things they could share and do. Holly was opening a whole new world to Kristian, and for the first-time life felt good.

Chapter Four

Kristian returned to his billet just in time to hear the British Lancaster Bombers flying overhead on their way to Germany. The sight and sound of the aircraft gave Kristian a terrible feeling, having to watch passively as they flew undisturbed on their way to cause the utter destruction of his homeland. He remorsefully walked into the building with his head hung low, wondering how many more friends and family would die a horrific death this evening while he lounges around his warm comfortable billets.

"Mail call," a young SS recruit shouted as he walked in the door carrying a small mailbag containing long desired letters from home. The young men gathered around the mail carrier eagerly awaiting their name to be called in hopes of some news from home. Kristian lay on his bed with his hands folded behind his head, indifferent to what was going on.

"Hey, don't you want to see if you got a letter?" Schmidt, Kristian's bunk buddy, said him.

"No, I don't have anyone left to write me anymore. They're all gone now," Kristian said starring sadly at the ceiling.

"Okay buddy. Tell you what. If I get a letter, I'll share it with you. It'll be like we both got one," Schmidt said, patting Kristian on his leg in an attempt to cheer Kristian up a little. Then he sprinted off to join the other boys gathered in anticipation of some word from home.

"Wezel," the carrier shouted and from the middle of the crowd an arm was raised. "Pfromm," the carrier shouted and another arm was stretched in the air. "Schmidt," the carrier shouted. Young Schmidt eagerly raised his hand and waved as he burrowed his way to the front of the crowd of hopeful boys.

Schmidt ripped open his letter as he walked back to his bunk and began reading the letter along his way, smiling from

36

ear-to-ear. Kristian watch Schmidt walk back to the bunks smiling as he eagerly read his letter. But Schmidt's smile turned to a look of shock and disbelief at what he was reading.

"What's the matter Schmidt, is everything ok?" Kristian said very concerned for his friend.

"No. My parents' apartment in Berlin was hit in a bombing raid, and my father is missing," young Schmidt said in despair, staring down at the floor.

Schmidt wasn't alone when it came to receiving bad news from home. Wezel got word that his mother, his father and younger brother had been killed. Pfromm learned from his parents that his older brother was killed on the Russian front. Some of the other boys received news just as bad. The joy and excitement the boys had felt in receiving mail had left; there was no news from home for anyone, except hardship, hunger and death. It was becoming clear that soon there would be no home to go back to.

The rest of the evening until lights out was spent in relative silence. The quiet was only occasionally broken by the sound of another squadron of English Lancaster route to destroy yet another German city. The consequences of these events did not fill the young men with despair, rather a determination to become harder and apply themselves in the coming combat with all the force that could be mustered in order to bring about a change of fate for Germany.

The next morning the SS recruits were hurried into a briefing room in order to give them a picture of estimated enemy troops in England being assembled for the inevitable invasion of mainland Europe. An SS captain escorted by a gruff looking sergeant came and stood in the front of the briefing room. "Attention", the sergeant bellowed. The young recruits all stood up at attention. "Heil Hitler," the captain greeted the men, raising his arm in the traditional Nazi salute. "Heil Hitler," The recruits said in unison raising their arms returning the salute to the captain.

"Men, there's new information on enemy troop strength", the captain began to explain to the recruits. It is believed that the Americans and the English are gathering troops for an invasion of fortress Europe. The situation report is as follows. The total number of British and American units ready for action are 40-42 infantry divisions, 4 independent infantry

brigades, 9-10 tank divisions, 11 independent tank brigades, 2-3

airborne divisions and 7 paratroop battalions."

"It is believed that this is just the beginning of the

buildup," the captain said with a sense of concern on his face and

in his voice. "It is believed that the invasion will come at the

Pas-de-Calais, with a diversionary attack at Normandy. Our units

will continue training and at the conclusion of training we will

be receiving orders for the location we will be assigned to

counter the invasion. Men, we will stop the enemy and push

them back into the sea. Heil Hitler." The captain again saluted

the recruits then quickly walked out of the room.

Schmidt, sitting next to Kristian, nudged him in

his side to get his attention. "What the captain just said

doesn't sound to inspiring to me. The way it looks to me

we are barely hanging on as it is. If they have that many

troops and they're just beginning their build up, we're in

serious trouble," Schmidt said to Kristian with raised

eyebrows and a clear sense of concern on his face.

"Don't worry so much," Kristian said with confidence. There's no way the Allies can break through our beach defenses. It'll be just like the captain said, they will be pushed right back into the sea."

Before the young men were dismissed, another sergeant entered the room. "Men, we just got word that the British made a night drop of supplies to the Belgium resistance just north of the town of Geel. Grab your weapons and gear, then load up on the transport trucks waiting outside. You have five minutes, move out," the sergeant yelled. "Looks like it's going to be a good day," Schmidt said to Kristian.

"We are going to get out of training for the day, yea," Kristian said.

"And get the hell out of here for a little while and see some of the country." The boys smiled at each other in excitement and quickly scurried off to gather their weapons and gear.

Though Belgium was an occupied country, most of the Flemish population supported the Germans. There was a portion of the population that was neutral toward the occupation and a smaller group who were absolutely hostile. The latter part of the population had secret connections in England and were supplied with weapons, explosives and radios in an effort to support missions of sabotage against the Germans. Though the Belgium underground did cause some havoc to the Germans, none of it was of great consequence. Their efforts were merely a burr under the saddle of the German Reich.

The boys loaded up into the troop transport trucks and they began their journey to Geel. It was a very cool morning and the wind blowing on the boys in the back of the open aired truck made them huddle together. Pfromm, sitting just across from Kristian, began stomping his feet in an unsuccessful effort to warm himself. "Son of a bitch its cold," Pfromm complained as he hugged himself still stomping his feet. "It didn't seem this cold when we left."

"Hang on little girl," Kristian said. "It's only a couple of more kilometers and we will be there."

The transport trucks pulled to the side of the road about 2 kilometers north of Geel near a field next to a wooded area. The young recruits jumped down out of the back of the trucks,

41

relieved to be out of the cold wind. The unit was split into groups. Four men, consisting of Kristian, Schmidt, a sergeant, and a lieutenant were assigned the duty of stopping all traffic coming down the road. One platoon was to gather those in the area of suspected collusion and the rest of the men were to search the field and woods for weapons and explosives.

After an hour of stopping passing vehicles, questioning the occupants and checking each of their papers, Kristian stepped behind one of the transport trucks to relieve himself. A car with a man and woman inside pulled up to the checkpoint and Pfromm and the sergeant began questioning the occupants. The woman's voice coming from the car was vaguely familiar to Kristian. Curious as to whom it might be he peeked around the back of the truck as he was buttoning up his trousers.

Kristian couldn't quite make out who the woman was from where he was standing but he was sure that he knew that voice. He began to walk closer to the car, and once in sight to his delight and surprise discovered that it was Holly. The sergeant questioning Holly didn't believe her story that she and her cousin were just out for a morning drive to see the area and ordered

Holly and the man accompanying her out of the vehicle. A clear look of fear overcame both of their faces.

"Holly," Kristian yelled, smiling as he hurried toward their car. An instant look of relief came over Holly's face. "Hello Holly, it's wonderful to see you; what are you doing here?" Kristian said gleefully.

"Wait, you know these people Kristian?" the sergeant said a little surprised.

"Yes sergeant, Holly is a friend of mine."

The sergeant stood down and ended his questioning of Holly.

"What are you doing here?" Kristian said again.

The sergeant gruffly interrupted the conversation.

"If you two lovebirds want to talk, pull the car to the side of the road so we can keep this line moving."

Holly and the man she was with, got back into the car and pulled it over to the side of the road. Kristian walked over to the car and began talking with Holly through the driver's side window that was rolled down. "So, what are you doing here?" Kristian said.

"I'm here visiting my cousin, Henry. It was such a nice morning we decided to go for a little drive. What are you doing here?" Holly said leaning over Henry from the passenger seat in the car.

"Looking for weapons the British might have dropped last night," Kristian said. "Hi," he said as he held out his hand to shake Henry's. "I'm Kristian; it's nice to meet you." Henry shook Kristian's hand without a word, just a slight smile on his face that looked as if it took a major effort to do. "*Not a very friendly guy*," Kristian thought to himself but his attention quickly returned to Holly.

"I hate to have to say hi and leave Kristian, but we're running late and really should go," Holly said.

"Can we get together this Saturday around 9 a.m.? Perhaps we could meet at the café."

"That sounds perfect Holly, I'll see you then."

As the car pulled away, Kristian and Holly waved, smiling at each other until out of sight. Kristian turned around to walk back to the checkpoint area to resume his duties. Kristian looked up as he was walking and saw Pfromm, the sergeant and his lieutenant standing there staring at Kristian with mocking smiles on their faces. As Kristian reached his comrades at the checkpoint the sergeant put his arm on Kristian's shoulder and gave it a pat. "Okay, Romeo, it's time to get the woman out of your head; we have work to do."

The search for weapons and explosives dropped by the British in support of the Belgium underground was quite a success. Forty-eight cases of submachine-guns and accompanying ammunition, parachutes and radios were found in the wooded area north of Geel. Several suspected civilians were arrested for helping the enemy and unlawfully carrying weapons, including signaling pistols. In other areas, there were drops of more ammunition, explosives and other miscellaneous weapons. It was clear that the underground was preparing for some type of attack on the Germans, but what, when and where were unknown.

45

Chapter Five

Saturday morning came around and Kristian was fit to be tied with excitement about seeing Holly again. Kristian put his grey SS uniform on and his freshly polished Jack boots, which were so skillfully shined one could see their own reflection. He was primping in the mirror, combing his hair and checking his face for any possibly missed whiskers from his teenage weekly shave when Pfromm quietly walked up behind him. With both hands Pfromm quickly grasped the top of Kristian's head and kneaded Kristian's hair with his hands into a ruffled mess.

"Hey, stop that, you're an asshole," Kristian said, swatting Pfromm's hands away from his head.

46

"What are you getting all spruced for pretty boy, got a hot date with a little French whore?" Pfromm said, taunting Kristian.

"Unlike the women you happen to frequent with, Holly is not a whore," Kristian said.

"Well, well aren't we special? I didn't realize you had such high standards and refined taste. I guess a fine gentleman such as yourself is much too good for the likes of us and the whores we see," Pfromm brayed in order to get the other boys in the room to join in on his jeer.

The young recruits in the room began to laugh at the taunting Pfromm was giving Kristian. Kristian said to Pfromm's comment with a one finger salute and returned his attention back to the mirror to recomb his hair.

Once Kristian was satisfied with the results of his primping in preparation to meet Holly, he quickly grabbed his garrison cap and practically trotted out of the barracks, whistling as he headed toward the door. The rest of the boys in the room all looked at Kristian, then each other, smiling at what they perceived as Kristian showing both silly and foolish behavior. A relationship between a pure Aryan German male and a little French girl could not be taken seriously and could only be looked at as a convenient and fun way to relieve a young soldier's tension.

Kristian arrived at the little café a few minutes prior to the scheduled rendezvous. Kristian sat down at an open table designed for two and nervously began to wait for Holly's arrival. He looked around the room and noticed a man who looked vaguely familiar reading a paper in the corner of the other side of the room. The man kept looking over his paper at Kristian as if he was not pleased with Kristian's presence at the cafe.

The man's strange behavior and familiar looking face, began to tweak Kristian's curiosity, so he stood up from the table and began to walk over to him. But he had hardly taken a step when he felt the light touch of a woman's hand on his arm.

"Kristian," Holly said in a pleasantly delicate voice. Kristian turned to Holly and his face instantly beamed with a smile from ear to ear and Kristin quickly forgot about the familiar looking man in the corner of the room.

"Holly, hi. It's wonderful to see you," Kristian said, smiling like a child on Christmas morning.

"It's good to see you too," Holly said returning the smile.

"Please, sit down," Kristian said as he pulled out a chair from the table for her to sit in. Holly began to sit at the table and Kristian slid the chair in behind her.

"Quite the gentleman," Holly said. "Is the German army finally teaching their soldiers some manners?"

"I'm in the SS Holly, not the army," Kristian said with just a touch of frustration in his voice.

"We are much more civilized in the SS."

"That is not what I hear about the SS," Holly said with a little sass.

"Let's not start off like this," Kristian said "Let's talk about something else. Would you like some coffee?" Kristian raised his arm and flagged down the waitress that was walking by and ordered the both of them a cup of coffee.

Good coffee was hard to come by due to mandatory rationing, and sugar with the coffee was completely out of the question. All a customer could expect their coffee to be was hot and black, if they could get any coffee at all. "So, Holly, what would you like to do today? We can do anything you want to do," Kristian said eager to please her.

"I think I would just like to walk around and talk. It's such a beautiful day and there's no better way to get to know someone other than talking to each other. How does that sound?" Holly said.

"That sounds wonderful," Kristian said willing to comply with any request Holly may have. "Any particular place you would like to walk to?" he said.

"No," Holly said with a smile hugging Kristian's arm, looking up into his eyes as in admiration of a hero. "I just want to enjoy you and this beautiful day."

Kristian lovingly smiled back at Holly and said, "Okay, we will do anything you want." Kristian and

Holly walked out of the small café hand in hand gazing at each other with smiles of utter joy on their faces. The day was bright and sunny, warm with a cool breeze in the air. As they walked, Holly held on to Kristian's arm tightly resting her head on his shoulder.

"Holly," Kristian said, "I've something to tell you but you have to promise to keep it to yourself and not tell anyone."

"I promise Kristian, I won't say a word. What is it?"

"We have orders to move out in a couple of days. My division is going to be relocated to Normandy, I hear near the town of Dreux. We are going to load men and equipment on the train and leave for Normandy on the 1st of April."

"That's amazing; I live near Dreux, Holly said Actually, between Dreux and Caen, but still, not too far from Dreux. I live in a town called Falaise. It's funny, I was having a hard time thinking about returning home tomorrow."

"That's wonderful," Kristian said with excitement. "We can see each other when I get situated at our new duty station."

They stopped in front of a small store and Holly admired a dress in the display window. "Oh Kristian, that dress is beautiful," Holly said, wishing she could have it. "I hope I can have a dress like that one day."

"I'm sure you will," Kristian said, smiling down at Holly. "It would look beautiful on you too, that's for sure." Holly smiled at Kristian then noticed two young women looking at Kristian, blatantly drooling over him from inside the store. Holly pulled Kristin down by the back of his neck and gave him a long passionate kiss making it very clear to the other women that Kristian was hers.

"Wow," Kristian said with surprise. "Not that I'm complaining, but what was that for?"

"I just wanted you to know that I was fond of you, that's all," Holly said as if it was just a small trivial gesture.

Kristian smiled at Holly and then arm in arm continued on their walk, strolling down the quiet streets on a lovely spring day. After an hour of roaming Kristian spotted a large tree in a secluded grassy area with plenty of shade to shelter them from the brilliant sun. "Let's sit under that tree and rest for a while," he said as he pulled Holly in the direction of the tree.

"Okay," Holly said, surprised by Kristian quickly pulling her in a new direction with a slight jerk of her arm.

They sat leaning against the trunk of the big old oak tree and began petting each other. As Kristian leaned back on the tree Holly sat up on her knees and placed her hands on both sides of Kristian's cheeks. Holly began kissing Kristian with quick and short but delicate kisses, and soon their kisses grew more and more intense as the passion for each other grew. Their desire for each other was nearly unbearable, and it was as if their bodies pressing against each other was not enough, they had to become one.

Kristian and Holly made sweet, soft and passionate love to one another for hours under the big old oak tree, discovering each other for the first time. As the thirst of the intimate touch of each other's body was quenched, Kristian and Holly laid on their backs in the green grass looking into the blue sky, telling each other what the white fluffy clouds resembled to them. Out of the corner of his eye, some movement caught Kristian's attention. A man was standing at the corner of a building a few hundred meters away and when the man noticed that Kristian had spotted him, he ducked back behind the corner of the building out of sight.

Kristian immediately knew that he had seen that man before, the familiar looking man from the café. "Hey, it's that guy from the café," Kristian said as he began to get up to go confront the strangely familiar looking man. Holly quickly grabbed Kristian's hand, holding him back from leaving. "Don't worry about him sweetheart, he'll go away. Let's just sit here and enjoy each other for a few more minutes, I'll have to go back to the house soon," Holly said.

Kristian complied with Holly's request and sat back down beside her. "I know I'll not be able to see you for a few days, I'm going to miss you," Kristian said sincerely.

"I'll miss you too," Holly said. "but, we'll get to spend a lot of time together once we both get to France."

"Holly," Kristian said. "I've never felt like this about any other girl before. I don't want to scare you off but, I think I'm in love with you."

"I know," Holly said with a smile and a raise of her brow. "I'm a hard girl not to love." Kristian looked at Holly a little surprised at what she had said and snickered. "Just kidding silly. It's okay, I feel the same way about you. I don't think I've been happier in my life. I've always wanted to be in love, to have my prince charming, and I've finally found him. Now I finally can say to someone, I love you too and really mean it."

Kristian and Holly talked a little longer about their dreams for the future and what they would like to do, both with each other and their own individual accomplishments. The time passed by and soon it was time to walk Holly back to her uncle's house. The young couple walked slowly back to the house and exchanged sorrowful goodbyes. They both knew that though their parting would not be for a long time, each minute apart would feel like an eternity.

Chapter Six

The Allies were debating the need to destroy the railway lines in France before the invasion of Europe in order to isolate the Normandy area, hindering movement of German reinforcements. Churchill initially feared the large number of French casualties that would result from such raids but later decided that these losses had to be made for the greater good. Included in the plans of preparation of the invasion were orders for the French Resistance to conduct sabotage operations against railway lines.

Whether or not they received orders from Britain, some members of the French Resistance were active already. The main line between Lille and Brussels was a target due to information

57

received by spies of the movement of the 12ᵗʰ SS division

expected that day through the area. On the night of April1st, the

resistance planted bombs and destroyed the rail line near the

small village of Ascq, close to the Belgian boarder, just as the

12th SS Panzer HJ Division was en route, causing a delay of

troop movements.

The train transporting the 12ᵗʰ SS was approaching

Ascq, a railroad junction where three railroads intersected. The

explosion blew the rail line apart, causing two cars to derail.

Although there were no casualties on the train, reprisals against

local residents, even if they had not been involved in the

sabotage, were conducted to deter further acts of sabotage.

There were no considerations for the innocent civilians by the

12ᵗʰ SS, anyone who got in their way or hindered them was a

target and many would pay with their lives.

The commander of the convoy, SS *Obersturmführer*

(lieutenant) Walter Hauck, ordered troops to search then arrest

all of the male members of the houses on both sides of the tracks.

They were guarded by German soldiers and were to be executed

by firing squad immediately. The civilians were beaten by the butts of the riffles by the SS solders and kicked as they lined the men up to be executed. Kristian was one of the troops assigned to execute the men beside the railway and he had no qualms with being part of the execution. This was being done for the Fuhrer and the Fatherland and for the betterment of the Third Reich, but Kristian was not an unsympathetic man and had at least some sense of compassion for these civilians.

The men to be executed were lined up and Kristian's platoon was given the order to take aim. Kristian wanted to make sure that his aim was true and accurate in order to make a clean kill and not to let his victim suffer. Kristian aimed his riffle at the head of a young boy no older than 16. Killing a man in combat was honorable, but killing someone like this, he was not so sure about. Though it was his duty, Kristian still felt a little uneasy about killing an unarmed civilian. The order to fire was given and Kristian fired his weapon. The round pierced the back of the young man's head and exploded out of the boy's face. The line of innocent men slumped almost in unison and fell to the ground with a muffled thud.

Another group of men were lined up in front of Kristian's firing squad, and the process repeated over and over until all of the civilians selected for reprisal were killed. Altogether 70 men were shot beside the railway line, and another 16 killed in the town of Ascq. Six other men were arrested, then charged with the bomb attack after an investigation by the Gestapo, and then they were finally executed by firing squad as well. The Mayor of Ascq, a Mr. Delebart, violently protested at the actions of the SS, the population having nothing to do with what had happened. The fact that they were innocent men made the Mayor extremely angry and fearlessly voiced his opinion. One of the young SS men began hitting the Mayor on the shoulder and said, "I've been ordered for you too to be shot as well," then gave a tremendous kick in the Mayors kidneys. Then he pushed him into another group of civilians who were awaiting execution.

After walking along the bottom side of the railway line for about 200 meters they came across the corpses of the men that were executed before them, then the command to halt was given. Kristian's platoon made them face the train line with their arms raised. The men knew that their time had come, and that they would be shot in the back, yet they stayed in that position for four to five minutes as if patiently waiting to be executed. A whistle sounded, it was the call of the conductor of the train alerting the soldiers to re-board the train and continue on to their destination.

Llieutenant Hauck, the officer in charge of the detail said in a loud voice to the civilian men in the line waiting to be executed, "You may put your hands down. Due to lack of time I, in the name of the Fuhrer, pardon you and release you to go home to your families." All of the prisoners looked at each other in disbelief and put their hands together in quick prayer in thanks for God's mercy, then without haste scurried back to their homes. "Men of the 12th SS all board," their sergeant shouted.

The young men of the 12th SS boarded the train and sat down in their seats to get ready for the long ride to their destination. Kristian sat down next to a young man named Karl Odt. Odt was 17 and a hard-core Nazi who believed that anyone who was not an Aryan should be exterminated. "Odt, what do you think about that?" Kristian said just to strike up a conversation.

"Think of what," Odt snapped, not wanting to talk.

"Executing those Frenchmen, what do you think?" Kristian said with a frown.

"Personally, I don't give a shit. If you fuck with the Reich you deserve to die. We are trying to make the world a better place with order and a stronger superior race; they're just like bugs to be squashed. The Reich has a great destiny and one day we will rule the world."

"*Wow*," Kristian thought to himself. "*This guy sounds like a propaganda pamphlet.*"

Kristian didn't reply to Odt's comments; he figured that there was really no point in talking to him. He would just get more of the same conversation that consisted of blind obedience to the Nazi ideology and not an ounce of individual thought. Kristian sat back and thought about what had just taken place at Ascq. He felt as if he was in the right and doing his duty, yet still felt remorse and a slight sense of shame. This is not the way he was taught to feel, this was not how a man of the SS was supposed to be, and Kristian was confused.

The steady repetitive sound of the smokestack chugging as the train moved down the track was soothing, and overpowering Kristian's ability to stay awake. It had been a long and exhausting day, and the tired and confused young man quickly drifted off to sleep. A few hours later Kristian woke abruptly to the sound of the steel wheels of the train screeching as the train slowed to a stop at their destination. Finally, they could get off of the train and discover where their new home was.

The young SS men were lined up in formation beside the train, then marched to their new billets, all of them excited to start their new adventure in France. Gotz Oden, another young recruit in the SS HJ, was marching alongside Kristian to the new billeting area, humming as he walked. Kristian had glanced over to Gotz and did a double take noticing the silly smile on his face. "What the heck are you so happy about, Gotz?" Kristian said, a little puzzled at Gotz's almost giddy looking face.

"I'm going to find me a sweet little French girl and never let her go. That French accent just drives me crazy," Gotz confessed.

"I understand," Kristian said. "It does a little something for me too."

The boys smiled at each other then continued on their march, both anxious to get a good night's sleep in their own beds. The unit reached the billeting area and the young men were assigned quarters. It was approximately 1 a.m. when they were allowed to crawl their tired bodies into their bunks, but their slumber would be short lived due to a formation at 4 a.m. for briefing on their new assignment. "God, I'm not going to make it, Kristian," Gotz said. "I can't make it with that little of sleep." Gotz gave Kristian a crooked smirk and fell face first on his bunk and was asleep before Kristian could crawl into his own bunk.

The next morning Kristian and the other men were awakened to the sounds of whistles, screaming NCO's and a metal trashcan being kicked across the floor of the room. Kristian, in shock at all the sudden commotion along with the other young SS men, immediately jumped out of bed and began quickly dressing in their uniforms. Kristian looked over to Gotz's bunk and unbelievably he was still asleep. "Wake up sweetheart, it's time to go to work," Kristian said, shaking Gotz. Gotz didn't wake or even move and inch, so Kristian grabbed the thin mattress Gotz was sleeping on and lifted it rolling Gotz on to the floor, immediately waking him. "What the hell did you do that for?" Gotz said angrily.

"It's time to get up dumbass, we have formation in about two minutes," Kristian told Gotz as he was buttoning his trousers.

Gotz rolled his eyes, gave a heavy sigh then rubbed his face with his hands still sitting on the floor.

"You better get your ass dressed or you're going to be late for formation," Kristian told Gotz with a very serious expression on his face.

"Yeah, yeah, I'm getting ready," Gotz said.

Kristian quickly grabbed the rest of his uniform, dressing himself as he walked out of the billets and into formation. Once all the young men were in formation the

Unterfeldwebel (Staff Sergeant) called the men to attention and the company commander, *Hauptsturnführer* (Captain) Wise, began to brief the young SS *Mannschaften* (enlisted men). Captain Wise was well known as a fearless warrior of the Third Reich, and it was an honor for the men to serve under him. All the men were excited to hear what the Captain had to say. Captain Wise stood almost regally in front of the men, you while sternly looking up and down at the line of boys as in a quick inspection of his troops, then began to speak.

"Men of the 12th SS HJ Division," Captain Wise said with unquestionable authority. "We have been assigned the honor by our Fuhrer to defend fortress Europe from invasion by the Allies. Command believes the expected invasion will be soon at hand, and it is believed that the invasion will come at the Pas De Calais with a diversionary attack here in Normandy. The defense of Normandy and the town of Caen is our assignment and the Fuhrer himself has chosen us for this mission. Train well men, the Allies have had a lot of time to prepare for the invasion. They have massed large amounts of men and weapons. It's going to be a hell of a fight."

Chapter Seven

Captain Wise continued with briefing of the men concerning the inevitable invasion of the Allies. "General Marcks has considered that there are two possibilities that can occur if the Allied invasion is at Normandy," the Captain said. "The first scenario would be a landing between Orn and Vire as well as the East of the coast of Cotentin with the objective of capturing Paris. The second possibility would be major landing east and west of Cotentin, with an objective being the capture of the harbor at Cherbourg."

"Our division's directive is to train and prepare for three plans of advance for a possible invasion in Normandy," Captain Wise said. "The first is crossing the Seine River between Paris and Rouen for action between the Somme and the Seine Rivers. The second would be the deployment between the mouths of the Seine and Orn rivers and the third being the deployment west and northwest of Caen. Men," Captain Wise said pointing his finger at his troops as if poking his finger on someone's chest. "We will practice each scenario until we can do it in our sleep, and when the enemy lands we will push them right back into the sea. Good luck men. That is all, you're dismissed."

The platoon sergeant then stood in front of the recruits and began to speak to the men. "Troops," the Sergeant bellowed. "The rest of your training is going to be a bit challenging due to the lack of supplies and constant Allied air raids. Troop transport and Panzer movements will be kept to a minimum due to the shortage of fuel. All fuel that can be obtained is being used by our valiant men on the Eastern Front. Much of our infantry training, troop movements and Panzer training will be conducted at dusk and night hours due to constant daylight bombing and strafing by the Allied aircraft."

"This training will be conducted three days a week with the rest of the days being exclusively utilized for training in fighting airborne enemy forces after a landing. Frequent practice alarms will be conducted to increase the speed of combat readiness of our units. Because of the expected landings by the Allies, we will set up defenses on all sides of the camp increasing our ability to repel any attack by Allied airborne troops. Return to your billets and get in full battle dress, then go to the armory and get your weapons. We will be conducting combat training with live ammunition today. That's all boys, move out."

The young recruits scattered like flies as they all scurried back to their respective billets to get their battle gear for the day's training. As Kristian and Gotz ran the boys smiled at each other and giggled like schoolgirls with excitement. "I can't wait," Gotz said to Kristian. "We are finally going to get some real training. I bet it's going to be fun as hell from here on out."

"Maybe training will," Kristian said. "But I bet when the Allies land it's not going to be so much fun."

"Don't be such a killjoy," Gotz told Kristian giving him a light shove on his shoulder as they ran. "Let's just enjoy it while we can."

The young recruits quickly retrieved their gear and weapons then returned out in front of their billets and lined up for formation, ready to be marched to the firing range where they were to conduct their training. "Attention," the Sergeant shouted to the young troops, and in unison the young boys instinctively and smartly snapped to attention. "Right face," the Sergeant then shouted and the boys quickly followed his command. "March." As the boys of the 12th SS marched to training, the Sergeant began singing an SS marching song and the boys joined the Sergeant in song. The song was called the "*SS marschiert in Feindesland* or *Teufelslied*," roughly translated, "The Devil's Song." And with a deep gruff sounding voice the sergeant began to sing.

SS marches in enemy land,

And sings a devil's song.

70

A rifleman stands on Volga's beach,

And silently hums along.

We care about nothing around us,

And the whole world can

Curse or praise us,

Just as it pleases.

Wherever we go we go always forwards!'

And the devil merely laughs,

Ha, ha, ha, ha, ha!

We fight for Germany,

We fight for Hitler,

The Red (Communism) will never get to rest.

We fought before in several fights,

In North, South, East and West.

And now we stand ready to fight

Against the red plague.

SS will not rest, we annihilate,

Until no one disturbs Germany's fortune.

And even if our line thins,

For us there's no going back.

Wherever we go, we go always forwards!

And the devil merely laughs,

Ha, ha, ha, ha, ha!

We fight for Germany,

We fight for Hitler,

The Red will never get to rest.

Once the recruits reached the training range they were divided into squads. The Waffen SS Panzer Grenadier platoon had three 12-man squads, each armed with two light machine-guns and an assortment of rifles, submachine-guns, and assault rifles. Lots of firepower. The range was approximately 200 meters long and 50 meters wide. On the left and right sides of the range there were two heavy machine-gun positions firing live ammo over the heads of the young recruits. The objective was to low crawl 100 meters into a good firing position in order to hit cardboard cut-out targets at the far end of the range.

Kristian's squad was the first squad to line up at the start of the course to make an assault. For the first 100 meters the young men had to low crawl the entire distance, while inches above them razor sharp barbed wire accompanied with heavy machine-gun fire whizzing by for a realistic effect. All of the young warriors had their weapon in hand, eager and ready to attack their enemy and prove their abilities as soldiers to go their superiors.

The platoon sergeant raised his right-hand signalling Kristian's highly motivated squad to ready themselves to begin their assault on their cardboard adversary. The sergeant quickly dropped his arm, simultaneously blowing a whistle signalling the squad to begin their attack. The young men dove to the ground from a standing position and began low crawling under the barbed wire toward their targets. The ground was dirt, no grass, and the dust rose from the ground into their mouths and eyes making them water to the point that actually seeing something was rather difficult at best.

Both machine-guns opened fire like a soldier covering fire against the enemy, the deadly rounds whistling just above the young recruit's heads giving them just a feel of the reality of the situation they would soon be in. About half way down the range there was a small gully that ran across the training grounds filled with mud and dirty water. The boys well knew that as an infantry soldier staying clean was not in the job description. It was expected by the boys, and almost looked forward to, just for the fun of getting filthy. Being a boy has its perks.

The boys crawled down into the gully through the mud and water, getting themselves satisfyingly muddy, then back up to the dusty dirt-filled course and continued low crawling to their firing positions. Once all of the boys had reached their firing positions, the squad leader gave the signal to open fire on their cardboard cut-out targets. The boys opened up with all they had, raining hell with rifle and submachine-gun fire upon their cardboard enemy. The divisional commander, *Bregade-Fuherer* (One-star General) Witt, was watching the training and applauded.

Once all of the young men completed the course, they were all invited by the general to come to the castle that the general had appropriated for use as his headquarters. In appreciation for the excellent results of the training and the highly motivated actions of his men, they were to be rewarded with cakes and coffee in the ground level hall of the castle. The

74

hall was filled to the brim with men, including recruits, the instructors, and the general himself. Kristian and another recruit named Gunter Krause, known to all of the boys as Gunny, were sitting on the castle hall floor leaning against the ancient and cold stone wall.

"This is nice," Gunny said as he was devouring his cake. "I haven't had anything like this since I left home. It's not quite as good as momma's but it's pretty good. I think I know what I want to be now; I want to be a general. Those guys have it made, and they live like kings."

"That they do," Kristian said. Gunny noticed that Kristian wasn't eating his cake, he had just sat the saucer with the cake on the floor and was for the most part just staring off into space.

"Hey," Gunny said, giving Kristian a nudge with his elbow. "You okay?"

Kristian looked at Gunny with a slightly forced smile and said "Yes, I'm just doing some thinking."

"What about?" Gunny said curiously.

"Just thinking about my girl," Kristian said.

"She back home?" Gunny said as he continued to eat his cake.

"No," Kristian said. "Actually, she's here."

"In France?" Gunny said with a little confusion on his face.

"Yes, she is a French girl and she lives between here and Caen."

"You're a lucky man," Gunny said. "You can see her within a couple of hours anytime you would like."

"That's right," Kristian said with a smile. "And I'm going to see her tomorrow." Gunny returned Kristian's smile and quickly went back to devouring his cake. "Hey," Gunny said nudging Kristian with his elbow and his mouth full of cake, "are you going to eat your cake?"

"No," Kristian said. "I'm not really hungry."

"Can I have it?" Gunny said as if he hadn't eaten for days."

"Go ahead little piggy," Kristian said jokingly. "We can't have you dying of starvation, now can we?" The boys smiled at each other and Gunny quickly snatched up the cake Kristian had given him.

"What's your girl's name?" Gunny said, just trying to keep the conversation going to help kill some time.

"Her name is Holly, and she is beautiful," Kristian said proudly.

"Hey," Gunny said with excitement as he sat up away from the wall and turned to face Kristian. "Do you think she might have a friend for me?"

Kristian looked at him with a playful frown as if he thought Gunny was in idiot. "Of course, she does, she's a girl, isn't she? Girls always have five or six friends."

"That's great," Gunny said with excitement.

"Hey, don't get too excited buddy, we don't know if any of them like ugly guys like you."

"With odds like that, one of them is bound to like ugly guys," Gunny said laughing.

Kristian started laughing as well. "You're probably right, between all of those girls one of them would have to. Tell you what," Kristian said. "I'll ask Holly tomorrow when I see her if she thinks she has a friend that might be willing to meet you."

"Fantastic," Gunny said with bated breath. "I'm going to meet me a little French girl, I'm going to meet me a little French girl," he said with a little tune in his voice.

"Take it easy boy," Kristian told his anxious friend, I have to ask her first."

"It's ok," Gunny said. "I have a good feeling about this. I'm going to get me a little French girl," Gunny began to sing again, bobbing his head and swaying his body from side to side, smiling ear to ear.

"Ok Romeo," Kristian told Gunny. "Just calm down and eat your cake." Gunny smiled at Kristian, then went back to eating his cake. Kristian was just as excited

78

about going to see Holly tomorrow, but he wasn't one of those guys who wore his emotions, whether good or bad, on his sleeve. Not that he couldn't show joy or pain, but Kristian truly believed that it was important for a man to keep his composure at all times, and completely undignified not to.

Chapter Eight

The next morning Kristian woke early to get a head start on his journey to see Holly in Falaise. He quickly got himself dressed and headed to the road outside of the compound. At the camp entrance, Kristian was met by two very large and unfriendly-looking guards. "Papers please," one of the guards demanded with a growl and a scowl on his face. Kristian quickly handed his identification papers to the guard. "Where is your pass, recruit?" the guard said Kristian.

"I'm sorry, here you are," Kristian said as he handed the guard his pass papers. "They seem to be in order," the guard said.

"Carry on." then waved Kristian to pass through the gate.

Kristian took his papers back from the guard, giving the guard a smile. The guard did not return Kristian's smile and, as a matter of fact, looked kind of pissed that Kristian had a pass while he was stuck pulling guard duty. Kristian's smile quickly left his face as he took the papers, with head held down began to walk out to the road. As he walked he thought to himself about what a grouch the guard at the gate was, then concluded that he too would have probably had a bad attitude if the roles were reversed.

Kristian continued walking down the dirt road toward Falaise, and after a few minutes a supply truck came driving from behind him. Kristian heard the truck coming, so he turned around to face the truck and said to himself, "Hey, maybe I can flag this guy down and catch a ride, instead of wearing out these boots." Kristian stood almost in the middle of the road waving his arms in the air. The driver slowed the truck and stopped the vehicle right next to Kristian. Kristian looked in the window of the passenger door and inside the cab sat a 16-year-old boy smiling from ear to ear.

Kristian wondered to himself if it would be a good idea to catch a ride with this boy. The boy's eyes were spread wide apart and his ears stuck out like a monkey, with a bit of an overbite and freckles above his cheeks. Kristian stood there silently staring at the boy. "Well?" the boy said, a little confused by Kristian's silence. "Are you wanting a lift or not?"

"Uh, yeah," Kristian said, then opened the passenger door and climbed into the cab of the truck.

The young boy struggled to put the Mercedes-Benz L3000 supply truck in first gear, grinding a little as he worked the stick into position. Kristian was watching the boy, a bit apprehensive and once again questioning if it was a good idea to catch a ride with this boy. "Where are you headed?" Kristian said the young driver.

"I'm headed to Caen," the boy said. "How about you, where are you going?"

"Well," Kristian said. "I'm trying to get to Falaise. Are you going near there?"

"This is your lucky day," the boy said. "I'm going right through Falaise."

"My name is Oscar, what's yours?" the young private said.

"My name is Kristian," Kristian replied, staring out the front windshield halfway day dreaming about seeing Holly.

"Nice to meet you," Oscar said. "What are you going to do in Falaise, not a lot going on there?"

"I'm going to see my girl," Kristian replied, looking at Oscar with a smile.

"A French girl, huh?" Oscar said with a cat-that-ate-the-canary smile. "Better be careful, those French girls sure can be trouble. I've heard a lot of stories about our boys getting mixed up with some little local tart; from what I hear they're nothing but trouble. Don't let that sweet smile and sexy accent fool you, buddy."

"I'm not too worried about that," Kristian said with confidence. "Holly's not like that at all. I met her in

Belgium and I think it was love at first sight for both of us."

"Well, that sounds awful nice, but be careful," Oscar said attempting to give Kristian some good advice. "I hear those French girls can turn on you in a second if you piss them off, and before you know it, she'll trick you and hand you over to the partisans. The outcome is awful bleak after that, buddy."

"Don't worry your little head about it private, I think I have this under control," Kristian said with a slight smirk.

"Okay," Oscar said with an expression of assuredness. "But, don't say I didn't warn you."

The boys drove about two kilometers down the road and spotted a German Panzer tank sitting in the middle of the road. The crew of the tank was jumping off the tank and running away as quickly as their feet could carry them. Kristian and Oscar both looked at each other with a *what the hell is going on?* look on their faces when the Panzer exploded, throwing parts of the tank in every direction. The boys instinctively ducked down in the cab of the truck in fear, but just enough so they could still see out of the windshield.

Immediately after the tank exploded, the road in front of them erupted in explosions about a meter wide and about two meters apart, coming closer and closer to their truck. A Hispano Mk II cannon round ripped through the roof of the cab of the truck with the sound of a baseball bat hitting the hood of a car. The soldiers and vehicles on the road were being strafed by a British Hawker Typhoon, one of the Second World War's most successful ground-attack aircraft.

The Typhoon was armed with Hispano Mk II cannons, eight unguided air-to-ground rockets, and 2×227 kg or 2×454 kg bombs. One of the 20 mm rounds fired from the Typhoon sliced young Oscar completely in half just below the navel. Oscar, still alive after the round had hit him, was in shock. Looking down at the severed lower half of his body, his eyes were open wide as was his mouth, and his hands were up in the air as if he were saying, *what the hell is this*?

This wasn't the first time Kristian had seen what horrors war can bring; he had seen it before. The bombing raids conducted by the British aircraft at night and the Americans by day had given him plenty of exposure to the indiscriminate carnage war brings. Oscar was looking down at his missing lower torso and began panting quickly, hyperventilating from the shock of seeing what had been done to his body. An uncontrollable panic came over Oscar and he began to scream.

Kristian leaned over to Oscar and grabbed his head with both hands and gently pulled Oscar's face into his shoulder hugging him in an attempt to comfort the dying young man. "It's okay buddy, I got you," Kristian said, trying to comfort him. "We will get a medic and he'll fix you right up, you'll see, you'll be just fine." Oscar's panicked moans slowly began to dissipate and a quiet stillness came over him, life leaving the young man's body.

Kristian hadn't noticed before but the cargo in the bed of the truck had caught fire and began to burn intensely. Looking out of the window in the back of the cab Kristian saw that the cargo consisted of hand grenades, panzerfäustes and miscellaneous rifle and sub-machine-gun rounds. In a panic, Kristian quickly jumped out of the cab of the truck and ran down the road trying to get as much distance between him and the deadly cargo as possible.

Kristian was about 50 meters away from the truck when it exploded, the force of the explosion so intense it blew the cab of the truck completely of, coming to rest in a field on the right side of the truck about 20 meters away. Kristian fell to his knees, trying to catch his breath, heart pounding and his mind racing. He realized that it was only by the grace of God his life had been spared.

Kristian gathered himself and continued. As he walked down the dusty dirt road, smoke billowed from burning vehicles that had been strafed by the Typhoon. As Kristian walked past a burning Panzer tank he noticed one of the tank crew member's body was hanging halfway out of the turret of the tank. The lifeless upper half of his body dangled down the side of the turret, and his arms and back were on fire. It reminded Kristian of some twisted type of human candle. Then the sickening sweet smell of burning flesh began to fill the air, encouraging Kristian to move on.

He walked down the road passing burning transport trucks and tanks that had been hit by the Typhoon's powerful cannons. Bodies of dead German soldiers lie scattered around the vehicles, both on the road and strewn about in the ditches and fields running parallel to it. The death and carnage didn't affect him deeply as he was numb to the sight of mangled bodies from what he had experienced back in Germany from the allied bombing raids. The years of being bombarded by the Allies had hardened Kristian in both mind, and the heart.

A *Sonderkraftfahrzeug 251,* half-track armored fighting vehicle weaved around the bodies and destroyed machinery in the road approaching Kristian from behind. The sound of the screeching tracks rotating on the vehicle as it approached, grabbed his attention and he quickly turned to see where the sound was coming from. Knowing the poor visibility that the driver had from inside the tank, he wanted to make damn sure he was out of its way. Seeing that the sound was coming from a troop transport vehicle and not a tank, Kristian raised his hands to wave down the driver of the half-track in an effort to catch a ride.

The driver of the 251 stopped the vehicle beside Kristian in the middle of the road. "Hey," Kristian said trying to get the driver's attention.

"Are you guys going near Falaise?"

"Yes, we are. We are going right through there," the middle aged fatherly looking driver said. "Do you need a lift, son?"

"Yes sir, thank you," Kristian told the driver gratefully.

"You don't have to call me sir, son; I work for a living. Okay kid, hop in the back with the other men and I'll drop you off on the edge of town," the driver said with a smile.

"Thanks," Kristian said. Kristian quickly ran to the back of the vehicle and climbed aboard the half-track, aided by the hand of a clearly seasoned soldier sitting inside the bed of the truck.

"What's your name, boy?" the soldier said Kristian.

"My name is Kristian, what's yours?" Kristian said.

"My name is Gunter," the soldier said. "We're coming straight from the Eastern Front. It's going to be nice to get away from those damn Russians for a while and get some rest."

"Hey," Kristian said with surprise. "I've a friend named Gunter, but we call him Gunny. It's kind of a nick name."

Well I'm not surprised," Gunter said. It's a pretty common name."

"Is it as bad as they say in Russia?" Kristian said, curious as to if the horrors he had heard of about combat in Russia were true.

"It's even worse than they tell you," Gunter said. "They have an endless supply of men and weapons and no matter how many of those bastards you kill, they just keep coming. We are low on fuel, ammunition and food. And there's absolutely no air cover.

"We are screwed my young friend, unless we get some of those wonder weapons the Fuhrer keeps promising us. I would tell you even more, but I don't want to be shot for being a defeatist," Gunter said, certain of what would become of him if he didn't keep his mouth. "You say the wrong thing to the wrong person, and your next date will be with a firing squad. Or you might get lucky and they will ship your young butt back East, they need all the men they can get back there."

"That sounds terrible," Kristian replied. "I'm glad I've a nice safe duty station here in France. From the way you make it sound, compared to the Eastern front, France is a paradise."

"Oh, it is my friend, it is." Gunter said with a very serious look on his face.

Chapter Nine

A 251-half-track rumbled down the dirt road kicking up a trail of dust behind it, so thick it obstructed the view of anything behind. Seemingly, out of nowhere, a motorcycle sidecar combination recklessly came barreling around the left side of the half-track. When the driver of the 251 caught sight of the motorcycle speeding up beside him out of the corner of his eye, he immediately jerked the wheel of the 251 to the right, the quick change of the direction almost overturning the vehicle, nearly throwing Kristian and the other men seated in the bed of the half-track completely out of the 251 and into the road.

The half-track then slid off the road and into the ditch that ran alongside, violently ramming the front end of the vehicle into the other side of the ditch. This caused all of the men in the bed of the 251 to fly into and slam against the cab of the vehicle, one on top of the other.

As Kristian and the other men in the bed of the 251 got their composure, they could see a convoy of *Kubelwagens,* the German equivalent of an American Jeep, following the motorcycle on the road. As each of the *Kubelwagens* passed the 251 they could see the young *Heer* (regular army) soldiers laughing, whistling and pointing at their misfortune as each of the vehicles passed by their wrecked half-track. The rattled men in the half-track quickly said by flipping each vehicle the bird as they passed, accompanied by a long list of lewd suggestions.

Just as the last vehicle passed, two U.S. P-47 fighters began a dive on the convoy. The P-47's primary armament was eight .50 caliber machine-guns, and in the fighter-bomber ground-attack role it could carry five-inch rockets or a bomb load of 1,103 kg the P-47. This brought utter devastation on any German gun emplacement, transport vehicles or tank the Germans had.

Kristian and the other men in the half-track could see the vehicles in the convoy come to a complete stop in the road when they had spotted the two P-47's begin their diving run, looking to make a quick and easy kill. The soldiers immediately exited their vehicles and scattered like roaches when the lights come on in order to get a safe distance from the P-47's targets of opportunity.

"Get your asses out of the track and get to cover," Gunter franticly bellowed. Without hesitation each of the men in the 251 jumped over the sides of the vehicle and ran for cover just as the P-47's began to open fire on the convoy. As the .50 caliber machine-guns opened up, one after the other the *Kubelwagens* exploded, creating huge fireballs as the red-hot rounds from the P-47's guns hit their fuel tanks.

The strafing run lasted just seconds, then the two birds of prey quickly flew away toward England just as quickly as they appeared. Thick black smoke filled the air from the burning vehicles. Eighty percent of the convoy was destroyed, amazingly, there were no injuries. Kristian walked over to

Gunter with a slight look of confusion on his face. "Why did they hit us and just fly off like that?"

"Well, my little cherry," Gunter began to explain, "if you were paying attention you would have noticed that they were not carrying any bombs on their bellies."

"What does that have to do with anything?" Kristian said, not having any idea where Gunter was going with this.

"It means that they had already hit their targets and dropped their bombs. They were most likely headed back to England and were running low on fuel. They spotted the convoy and took a quick run at us on the way home. You can't blame the bastards, I would have done the same thing.

"Come on, kid," Gunter said to Kristian as he slapped him on the back of his helmet. "Looks like we have a walk ahead of us; we might as well get started.

" Kristian, following Gunter, jumped across the ditch and got back onto the dirt road. As they walked past the wreckage the P-47's had left on the road, the soldiers that had been riding in the vehicles were standing around smoking cigarettes. The men were laughing and joking about what had just taken place, trying to make light of the horror they had just experience and grateful to be alive.

The reactions of the men were quite calm, as if it were just another day on the job. The Germans had almost become complacent to such experiences due to the constant and frequent attacks by Allied aircraft. The Allies had total air supremacy by this time in the war, and the Germans had little aircraft left to deal with such attacks. Those aircraft that were available for defense were, for the most part, dedicated to fighting the Russians on the Eastern Front.

"How long have you been in the service?" Kristian asked Gunter as they walked down the road past the burned-out vehicles.

"I joined the *Heer* (Regular army) back in 1939 just before the invasion of Poland," Gunter said. "It seemed like a good thing to do at the time, but I had no idea I would be in a war six months later," Gunter said with a raised brow. "I had a nice cushy assignment in Poland after it surrendered and in 1940, when we invaded France while other units were getting shot at. Where was I? I was relaxing enjoying the spring in Poland. It was great, until Hitler decided he needed more *Lebensraum*, (Living-Space) for the Reich."

"Then," Gunter said with dismay, "on a beautiful Sunday morning in June of 1941 our Fuhrer decided to launch Operation Barbarossa and invade Russia. Why he thought that was a good idea I'll never know."

"You don't agree with our Fuhrer?" Kristian said, a little surprised at Gunter's reply and feeling a little angry that he would question the Fuhrer's decisions. "That's treasonous."

"Hey," Gunter said. "I'm all for getting rid of the Bolsheviks. Personally, I hate the bastards, but having a war on two fronts is not a very sound decision."

"Since then," Gunter continued "Hitler has declared war with the United States, adding another enemy to fight. We have lost North Africa, The Italian front is falling apart, Russia is a meat grinder that is now impossible to hold back, and now we have to worry about the imminent invasion of Europe by the Allies. Taking all of this all into consideration, doesn't it make you question Hitler's judgment just a little?"

Kristian looked at the ground as he walked, thinking about Gunter's question. Could his belief in the Fuhrer be misguided idolatry of a man who wasn't an infallible God, as his indoctrination into Nazi ideology had made him out to be? This new train of thought was confusing. Were these traitorous thoughts? Was Gunter spreading defeatism or was he right about Hitler and the war? Kristian found that Gunter's logic was hard to argue and he began to find himself, for the first time, thinking independently instead of having blind faith in what he was told.

"If that's what you feel why don't you quit, why don't you just desert and leave?" Kristian said, curious at what his answer might be.

"Oh no, my young friend," Gunter said slightly raising the pitch of his voice. "Not a chance. I think my chances are much better at the front than in front of a firing squad. You know what I would really like, kid?" Gunter said.

"What's that?" Kristian said.

"I would like to get me a nice little wound that would get me sent home. I would be a hero with a nice shiny medal from the war, and I would find me a nice quiet place out in the country to spend the rest of my days."

"That does sound nice," Kristian said. "But, don't you think it would be a great honor to die in battle for the Fuhrer and the Fatherland?"

"Oh, son," Gunter said shaking his head in disbelief at what he heard such a young man say. "There's no honor in dying; the honor is the staying alive to take care of those who depend on you. There lies the honor," Gunter said with the wisdom of age. "If it comes to the point of surrender or death, surrender. The

Allies will treat you okay. If they were Russians on the other hand, I would say you're better off just to die in battle. It's where you'll end up anyway, believe me it's quicker and there's a lot less suffering.

"Tell me, young Kristian," Gunter said. Do you have a girl back home?"

"Actually, Gunter," Kristian said with a smile. "I've one right here in France."

"Oh really," Gunter said a little surprised. "A little French girl huh? I can see you're the kind of man who gets right down to business," Gunter said jokingly with a fatherly smile.

"Yeah," Kristian said, smiling back at Gunter. "I actually met her back where I was training in Brussels. She was there on holiday and we went on a couple of dates. I later found out that she was from Falaise and that's where I'm heading now."

"I guess we'll have to pick up the pace," Gunter said with a smile, coaxing Kristian to walk a little faster. "We can't keep a lady waiting, now can we?" Kristian smiled back at Gunter and began in time and step with Gunter.

"So, Kristian," Gunter said. "What's the name of this young lady you're so eager to see?"

"Her name is Holly," Kristian said. "She is not just another girl; I really like her too."

"That's great," Gunter said. "Is she pretty?"

"Holly is beautiful, I really got lucky when I met her," Kristian said.

"Well, you're a lucky man," Gunter told Kristian. "Finding love is a wonderful thing. Many people go their whole lives and never find true love. You're one of the lucky ones, son; never take it or her for granted and it'll last forever. I was one of the lucky ones too," Gunter said smiling down at Kristian. "I met my Greta when we were both young and we are still together. I plan on growing old with that woman, so I can't go and get myself killed in this damn war. If you want to grow old with your girl, you had better keep your head down too boy."

"Yes sir," Kristian said to Gunter with a growing respect and admiration for the seasoned and battle tested man.

Kristian and Gunter continued their march down the road moving toward each of their individual destinations. As the two men walked, they continued small talk with each other occasionally joking and poking fun at one another, but Kristian's mind was truly on Holly. His anticipation to see her was almost to the point of being overwhelming at times, but it was better to keep his composure than to humiliate himself by looking like some love-stricken schoolgirl. Occasionally Kristian would smile to himself, thinking of seeing Holly soon, he kept telling himself. "Just a few more miles. Just a few, more, miles."

Chapter Ten

Kristian and Gunter, both tired and dirty from the long

walk down the dirt road, made it to the outskirts of Falaise.

"Well boy," Gunter said putting his hand on Kristian's shoulder.

"This is where we part ways. Let me give you a good piece of

advice son. Don't believe all of that Nazi Aryan supremacy crap

they feed you boys. We aren't any better than anyone else. It's

clear as a bell that we are not going to win this war and the only

thing you need to concern yourself with is keeping your ass alive

until it's over; you got that boy?"

Kristian wasn't sure if he believed Gunter or not, being

that it was contrary to everything he had been told, and at this

point still believed. Just due to the fact Kristian liked and respected Gunter he said with a smile, a nod of his head and a warm "Yes sir."

Gunter smiled and gave Kristian an affectionate pat on his shoulder and began to walk away. "Remember," Gunter yelled back at Kristian. "Keep your butt alive and marry that little French girl and name your first born after me."

Gunter gave Kristian a smile and waved goodbye over his shoulder. "Good luck, Gunter," Kristian yelled as he waved back to him. "I hope you get that wound and medal you're wanting." Gunter looked back over his shoulder and smiled at Kristian then turned back looking down the road to where his destiny lay. Kristian stood there in the road watching as Gunter walked away, pondering both of their futures and hoping Gunter got it safely through the war.

From the road Kristian could see Falaise Castle sitting imposingly on a raised rocky hill overlooking the town. Kristian loved historical places and castles were his favorite. The castle was William the Conqueror's built and in various phases during the 12th and 13th centuries, it was still a very sturdy fortress. The castle included three substantial keeps, the large central body to the castle, a small square tower, and a tall round tower with ditches both inside and outside the castle to provide additional defenses. Seeing the castle, Kristian quickly determined that he would take advantage of the opportunity of being in Falaise to visit the castle.

Kristian began to walk into the town to find Holly's home. Having an address, but not knowing the town, he needed to find someone that might be able to give him the directions to the street that Holly lived on. Kristian wandered the streets trying to find someone to ask, but it seemed as if the town was empty. A little confused, Kristian continued to walk the streets. As he neared the center of town he came upon an open market lining the street, filled with people buying vegetables, flowers and even a few farm animals like chickens and goats. Kristian spotted a friendly looking man at a table peddling cucumbers and melons so he decided to go over and ask him if he knew where Holly's street was.

Kristian walked over to where the old man was peddling his goods. "Melons, get your ripe, juicy melons," the old man was shouting over the noise of the shoppers.

"Sir," Kristian said tapping on the old man's arm trying to get his attention "Would you like to buy some melons?" the old man said.

"No sir," Kristian said. "I need to know where a street is located; could you please help me?"

The old man stood back and looked at Kristian with just a slight frown on his face. "Tell you what son, I'll help you, if you buy a melon," he said as his frown transitioned into a smile, knowing that he was about to make a sale.

"That sounds fair, sir," Kristian said. "Can you tell me where Rue Saint-Gervais is?" As the old man began to give Kristian directions to the street, something caught Kristian out of the corner of his eye. It was Holly in a white sun dress, angelically standing at a flower stand purchasing some fresh tulips.

Excited in seeing Holly, Kristian began to walk away from the old man when he was quickly grabbed by his arm.

106

"Oh no, where do you think you're going boy?" the old man said Kristian with a scowl on his face.

"I don't need directions now sir, thank you," Kristian said as he began to pull away from the old man's grasp.

"No, no, no, no, you still have to buy a melon," the old man demanded, tightening his grasp on Kristian's arm.

Reluctantly Kristian gave the old man some change to pay for the melon and began to walk away. Again, the old man grasped his arm and stopped him from leaving.

"What now," Kristian said the old man now getting a little frustrated with his refusal to let him get to Holly. "I paid you for the melon, what more do you want?"

"Relax son," the old man said, with a smile holding a melon in front of Kristian's face. "You forgot to take your melon." Kristian gave the old man a frown and snatched the melon with a quick sweep of his hand and turned to walk away to meet Holly.

As Kristian turned around to see Holly, she was no longer at the flower stand, and he frantically began looking around the market in an effort to spot her. Holly's white dress once again caught his eye, she was bent down admiring and cooing along with a baby just a few vegetable stands away. Kristian's frantic feelings turned to joy seeing Holly and a loving smile came over Kristian's face. Kristian walked over to where Holly was playing with the baby, silently standing beside her, watching as she lovingly played with the infant. Kristian's presence caught Holly's attention and she looked up to see who was standing next to her. Shocked at seeing Kristian's face, Holly quickly stood up with a beaming smile on her face. "Oh my God, Kristian, what are you doing here?" Holly said both surprised and excited to see Kristian.

"I got leave, so I decided to come see you," Kristian said. "I hope it's okay?"

"Okay? It's wonderful," Holly said. "I'm so glad to see you." Holly noticed the melon in Kristian's hand.

"Are you going to eat that?" she said as she pointed at the melon making a slight snarl expression on her face.

"Oh no," Kristian said shaking his head. "Here, this is for you," he said to Holly holding the melon up in front of her. "I don't know what they teach the boys back in Germany," Holly said, a little surprised at such a strange gift, "but in France it's customary for the boy to bring the girl flowers when he comes to call."
Kristian turned a little red and said, "No, no I…"

"It's ok silly," Holly cut him off in mid-sentence, "it's just as nice." "We are going to have to go somewhere. Everyone knows everyone here, and I don't want it getting back to my family that I'm talking with a German."

"Okay, Kristian replied, understanding the situation. Where can we go? Hey," Kristian said, excited at his idea. "Let's go up to the castle; I would really like to see it anyway."

"Okay," Holly said. "I just love that castle, it brings back a lot of memories from my childhood."

Holly grabbed Kristian by the hand and led him away from the market. Out of sight of the market and any curious onlookers, Holly stopped Kristian in the road. Holly threw her arms around Kristian's neck and pulled him into her lips, giving Kristian a long-awaited passionate kiss.

"Wow," Kristian said grinning as they each pulled away from their embrace. "If I knew I would get that kind of reception I would have come much sooner."

Holly cocked her head and looked at Kristian from the corner of her eye. "Is that all you want me for, my kisses?"

"No," Kristian said with a sheepish smile. "No, I want you for more than that."

The two young lovers continued their walk to Falaise Castle, holding hands along the way and repeatedly giving each other loving glances with devilish smiles that clearly told one another what was soon to come once a private moment could be had. The young couple reached the castle grounds, and Holly showed Kristian all the places her and her friends would play when she was younger and the silly things that happened during that time. Holly and Kristian laid down in the grass on a hill of the dried-out moat that surrounded the castle where they could relax, rest and talk.

"Kristian," Holly said.

"Yes," Kristian said.

"I've been trying to figure out a way to tell you, but I haven't figured out any other way than just come right out and say it," she said with a troubled look on her face.

"What is it, Holly? Just tell me it'll be okay," Kristian replied, trying to reassure Holly that anything she told Kristian would be okay.

"Well," Holly said, then let out a heavy sigh fearful to say what she had to tell Kristian. "I...I...."

"What is it?" Kristian said, trying to coax whatever it was out of her. "Just say it."

"I'm pregnant," Holly said.

Kristian, completely stunned at what Holly had just told him just laid there, his back propped up on his elbows and an expression like a deer in the headlights on his face.

"Kristian," Holly said, worried looking at the expression on Kristian's face. "Are you okay?"

"Uh yeah," Kristian said.

"Is that all you're going to say?" Holly asked, feeling a little upset by Kristian's response.

"No, I… that's just a shock to me. It's about the last thing I expected to hear you say, it's just, I…I…"

"Okay," Holly said. "I know it's quite the surprise, but what do you think? Are you happy?"

"Yes, of course," Kristian said still shocked at what Holly had told him.

"There's one problem Kristian," Holly said.

"What is it?" Kristian said sincerely concerned.

"I can't tell my family the father of my baby is a German; they will throw me out into the streets. I'll have to tell them that I got pregnant by a French boy and he left to go fight in the resistance."

Kristian didn't like the thought of not being able to acknowledge his own child, but he knew very well what her family and the public would do to her if they found out the child's father was German. They both sat up next to each other, side by side with one arm around one another. Holly tilted her head to the side, resting her head on Kristian's shoulder as they sat in silence.

Chapter Eleven

Kristian and Holly spent the rest of the day at the castle walking, talking and contemplating the lives they might have together. They walked hand in hand with a loving grip neither wanted to release. As the sun began to fall, Holly remembered that she needed to be home before sundown or she would be in trouble with her parents. "Kristian," Holly said stopping their stroll around the castle grounds with both sadness and reluctance on her face. "I have I to go home before dark, but I have you an idea how I can get out of the house later."

"What's this devious little plan you've come up with in that beautiful head of yours?" Kristian said with a smile.

114

"I'm going to tell my parents that I'm going to spend the night at a friend's house and that we are going to a party a family friend is having; since we will not be home until late this way she'll not have to walk home alone," Holly said with a bounce and a smile, proud of her genius plan that would get her back into Kristian's arms. "That is a pretty good plan," Kristian said. "This isn't something you do often with other boys, is it?" he said both joking and curious.

"No, you jerk," Holly said as she playfully slapped his face then turned to run home. Kristian stood there watching Holly run, holding his face with his hand where Holly had just slapped him. As he watched Holly run, she suddenly stopped and turned around to face Kristian. She hesitated for a moment then ran back to Kristian and gave him a quick little kiss on his lips then again turned and began running home. "Stay right here," Holly yelled back to Kristian as she ran. "I'll be back here in an hour or so,"

"Don't worry, I'll be right here waiting for you," Kristian yelled back to Holly." "Just don't take too long," Kristian smiled as he watched Holly run out of sight, but his smile faded away knowing that he would drudgingly count the minutes until her return.

Kristian slowly walked around the castle, occasionally kicking a rock thinking about the new situation that he was now in. He would no longer be the carefree young boy living just for himself, now he had a baby on the way. His needs or wants would no longer be top priority, now his child would have to come before everything. His whole existence would now be for the betterment of the beautiful gift that he would soon receive. Just after sunset Holly returned. She ran straight into Kristian's arms hugging him tightly. Kristian returned Holly's embrace, then some movement in the distance caught his eye. There was a dark silhouette of a man peering at Kristian and Holly.

"Holly," Kristian said as he separated her from their embrace, "do you see that man peeking around that building at us?"

Holly turned around to look at the man and strained to get a good look at the man. "That is odd, I wonder why he is watching us?" Holly said.

"I don't know but I'm going to find out," Kristian said as he pulled away from Holly, heading in the strange man's direction.

"No," Holly said, grabbling Kristian by the arm desperately trying to keep Kristian from leaving her. "Don't bother with him, I'm sure he'll go away. Come on, we have better things to do." She pulled Kristian away by his arm, distracting him from his curiosity.

Holly pulled him by the hand directing him to come with her, and he eagerly followed. "So," Holly said. "Where is your unit stationed; is it far away?"

"No," Kristian replied. "It's just a few kilometers away. Our unit is spread out right now in different locations for training, some stationed near Mailly, some in Garney and some of the lucky ones are near the Castle Coulonges. I don't think I'm supposed to

117

say exactly where my unit is though, that would be classified information and I could get in serious trouble."

"I understand sweetie," Holly said. "It's best I didn't know anyway,"

"We don't have much time together," Kristian said. "I have to head back in the morning, but we have tonight and we can make the best of it, if you know what I mean," he said with a devilish look on his face as he raised and lowered his eyebrows repeatedly.

"Oh, you're so bad," Holly replied, as she slapped Kristian on the chest with a smile on her face that stated she clearly understood what Kristian was implying, and was willing to comply with his carnal request.

The two young lovers walked until they found a secluded area, then sat down on the cool thick grass. Kristian reached over to Holly and brushed her hair out of her face, brushing his hand across the soft skin of her forehead. Holly leaned over to him and kissed his lips as soft as a whisper, then pulled away and stared into his eyes. "I love you, Holly,"

Kristian said with the most sincerity and passion Holly had ever experienced. Ferociously, like a bolt of lightning, Holly grabbed Kristian by the back of his head and passionately began to kiss Kristian as if to devour him.

Kristian was the first man Holly had ever lost her composure with, sharing with him her most secret desires. In a matter of seconds Kristin had Holly's dress up around her waist, his pants unbuttoned and his youthful virility deep inside her. Holly held Kristian tight, her legs wrapped around his hips bucking in time with Kristian's thrusts. Quickly, they drove each other higher and higher until they both grunted a primal moan in a simultaneous explosion of ecstasy. Exhausted from the intensity, Kristian and Holly then collapsed in each other's arms, completely drained by the nirvana they had both just experienced.

In between repeated sessions of making love, Kristian and Holly spent the rest of the night talking about their future, the wonderful life they would have together and how grand things would be after the war. Their youthful naivety hid the brutal reality of the situation that they were in, and the cost that would have to be paid for the insanity of the world that had been forced upon them. (For now, in their youthful eyes, the world was beautiful and full of opportunity, but the pleasure they now shared would soon turn to fear and desperation as the war comes ever closer, closing in upon them.)

A light morning dew covered the grass when Kristian and Holly awoke the next morning, both of them wet and shivering. Kristian put his grey M36 field tunic that they had been using as a pillow around Holly to shelter her from the morning chill, and rubbed her arms and back in an effort to warm her. "How is that, do you feel a little warmer sweetie?" Kristian lovingly asked.

"Yes, that feels very nice," Holly said. "I had better get home soon." "I know," Kristian said. "I have to head back too."

They got to their feet and embraced each other one last time before parting, not knowing how long it would be until they would once again be together. "I'll come see you as soon as I possibly can," Kristian said with both regret and sincerity on his face, and in his voice.

"Make it soon," Holly said, then stood on her tiptoes to kiss Kristian. "I love you."

"I love you too, Holly," Kristian said as he took his tunic from around Holly's shoulders.

Kristian and Holly both slowly began walking away holding each other's hand until the distance would no longer allow them to touch, looking back at one another as they parted until both could no longer be seen. As Kristian walked down the road he began to think to himself about what the future might hold for him. Would he survive this war? Would he and Holly have a life together in peace with a beautiful child that they had created together? The joy he had felt with Holly's company left with her and his mind now became weary of what may come to be.

After an exhausting trek back from Falaise, Kristian walked in to his billets and Gunny was sitting on his bunk polishing his jackboots to a glistening shine. Gunny looked up as Kristian entered the door. "Hey buddy, you made it back. How was it, did you have a good time?" Gunny said with a grin.

"Yes, you little pervert, we had a wonderful time," Kristian said as he threw his cap on his bunk and began taking off his tunic.

"Oh, tell me all about it, is she a little wildcat?" Gunny asked, eager to hear all the details.

"No Gunny, those are my memories; I think I'm going to keep them to myself," Kristian said undoing his tie.

"You're no fun," Gunny said with a frown.

"I would tell you all the juicy details if I had been with a little French tart."

"That's the difference between you and me, Gunny," Kristian said as he flopped his body down onto his bunk, resting his hands behind his head. "I'm a gentleman and I know how to be discrete when it concerns a lady."

"Well la tee da Mr. Fancy Pants, excuse me," Gunny said sarcastically as he threw his polishing rag at Kristian, hitting him in his face.

"Hey, are you hungry Romeo, let's go get some dinner," Gunny said.

"That sounds good," Kristian said. "I haven't eaten all day and I'm starving."

"Well let's get you something to eat," Gunny said sarcastically followed by a wink of his eye. "We have to make sure we keep your strength up for your little French girl." Kristian rolled his eyes and quickly hopped up from his bunk. As Kristian and Gunny began to walk out of the billets, Gunny put his arm around Kristian's shoulders. "Are you sure you don't want to tell me just a little about what you did to that sweet little French girl?" Kristian elbowed Gunny in his ribs and Gunny gave a loud chuckle as they walked through the door.

Around midnight Kristian and the rest of the boys of the HJ SS were awoken by the ear-piercing sound of air raid sirens. The entire unit quickly grabbed their weapons and half-dressed, ran outside to man their duty stations. Kristian and Gunny jumped into their foxhole, rifles in hand, peering into the night sky to see if they could catch a glimpse of the Allied aircraft.

Suddenly spotlights lit up the sky and the air raid sirens stopped

bellowing. The silence was almost deafening, but soon they

could hear the thundering sound of hundreds of Allied aircraft

approaching from the English Channel.

As the Allied aircraft came into range, the anti-aircraft

batteries opened fire in a desperate attempt to down any aircraft

that was unlucky enough to be lit up by the German spotlights. It

wasn't long until the whistling sound of death falling from the

air could be heard followed by repeated explosions one after

another headed their way. The sound of the explosions got closer

and closer and uncontrollable fear began to come over Kristian.

The two young men sat down in the foxhole burrowing

themselves as low as they could possibly get in an attempt to

save themselves from the oncoming horror of an aerial

bombardment. Bombs exploded all around them for what

seemed to be hours with no end in sight. The fear was

overwhelming, and enough to drive any man to the point of

insanity. Kristian and Gunny sat in the bottom of the foxhole

holding onto each other, both crying, their nerves shattered knowing death could come at any second and there was nothing

that they could do but wait for its arrival.

Chapter Twelve

The bombs stopped falling just as quickly as they began. Slowly, as Kristian and Gunny attempted to pull themselves together, they both stood up and peeked over the edge of the foxhole making sure the bombardment had ended before they crawled out. The devastation was unbelievable. The landscape, as far as they could see in the dark illuminated by the moonlight, looked like the lunar surface. What parts of buildings that were still standing were burning, just shells of what they once were.

"Holly shit," Gunny said in a loud voice. "I thought we were dead."

"What?" Kristian shouted, not being able to make out what Gunny had said due to the ringing in his ears caused by the loud explosions of the bombs.

"I said…" Gunny began to reply but was interrupted by Kristian.

"Let's go see if anyone needs help," Kristian shouted as he waved for Gunny to follow him. The boys split up, both looking around in the darkness trying to find anyone who might be injured and in need of aid.

Kristian went from crater to crater and everywhere in between trying to locate any wounded but was unable to find anyone. Kristian stopped walking and stood silently for a moment wondering why he couldn't find anyone after such an intense aerial attack. Kristian began to faintly hear someone calling out for help in the distance and ran in the direction of the desperate cries. Occasionally Kristian would have to stop and carefully listen in an attempt to hear the wounded soldier over his heavy panting from adrenalin and his frantic search.

Kristian finally found the young man who had been crying out for help lying on the ground in between two large bomb craters, terribly wounded but amazingly still alive. The boy's left arm was gone, and both of his legs had been completely blown off below his hips. Kristian knew that these wounds were fatal, and that there was absolutely no chance of this boy surviving. All Kristian could do was to stay by his side and try to comfort him the best he could until his inevitable death.

Kristian knelt down beside the boy and began running his fingers through the dying boy's hair and empathically patting the young man on his chest. "It's going to be okay," he said, trying to calm the boy down during his slow demise. "You're going home, you're going home to your family now." The boy was shaking uncontrollably and staring at Kristian with a clear expression of total fear on his face. Kristian continued to run his fingers through the boy's hair trying to keep a smile on his face as if everything was going to be fine.

"Tell me about your mom, tell me a memory of her," Kristian said to the boy.

"I... I remember her baking fresh bread," the boy replied, then winced in pain.

"Tell me about her bread," Kristian said trying to keep the boy's mind off of the excruciating pain.

"The smell," the boy said, "I always loved the smell of her freshly baked bread."

"It sounds wonderful," Kristian said.

"I can smell it, I can smell the bread," the boy told Kristian. Then his young broken body stopped convulsing and relaxed, his pain leaving his body accompanying his last breath.

Kristian sat there for a minute with the young boy's lifeless body. "I didn't even know your name," Kristian said with a look of confusion and remorse on his face. Kristian stood up and slowly began to walk away. No longer frantically looking for wounded men, but aimlessly walking around contemplating his own mortality, Kristian began to question himself. "Am I going to die a horrible death like that? Will I be all alone? Will no one know who I am and just bury my body in a hole somewhere?"

"Kristian," Gunny yelled as he was running up to Kristian. Gunny grabbed Kristin by the arm and pulled him around to face him. "Hey, Kristian. Are you okay?"

"Uh... Uh yeah, I'm fine," Kristian said with a blank yet confused look on his face.

"Hey, pull yourself together buddy. There's a lot of wounded over there that need our help. Come on," Gunny said, pulling on Kristian's arm coaxing him to follow. Kristian, at the pull of his arm, snapped out of his trance state and quickly ran off with Gunny to aid the other men in desperate need of help.

When Kristian and Gunny arrived at the area where all of the wounded men were, it was an anti-aircraft emplacement. There were bodies strung around, some without legs, some without arms and some completely blown in half. The sight was grisly but the boys had to spring to action. They had basic first aid training during their indoctrination into the SS but nothing prepared them for something like this.

The boys didn't have any bandages or anything to lessen the pain for the wounded men so they took off their shirts and ripped in strips to use them as tourniquets and bandages for the wounded men. Gunny ran over to where Kristian was wrapping a wounded young soldier's leg. "We have got to get some help for these men or they're not going to make it, I'm going to run over to the medical building and try to get some help." Kristian nodded ok to Gunny and turned his attention back to the wounded men.

The wounded young man that Kristian was trying to put a tourniquet on had lost part of his right leg from the knee down. The young boy raised his head from the ground and said to Kristian with a shaky and frightened voice. "Am I going to die?" "No...no," Kristian said with a smile, trying to calm the young boy. "You're going to be fine. This isn't enough to kill you but it'll get you sent home."

"Damn it," the young boy said angrily.

"What's wrong?" Kristian said.

"I wanted to die in battle, like a true warrior," the boy said, very disappointedly.

"Well that's not your destiny; you're going home," Kristian said to the boy. "I've got to go help the other men, don't run off now, okay?" Kristian said with a smile and lightly slapped the boy on the cheek and quickly ran off to help the other wounded men.

The night slowly passed, as Kristian and the other troops that were not wounded from the aerial bombardment worked through the night, trying to save as many of the wounded men as possible. By morning Kristian was exhausted from the lack of sleep, the intense adrenalin rush, and the running from wounded man to wounded man. Gunny and Kristian found each other and sat down together and leaned on the wheel of a destroyed Kübelwagen, to rest.

"I'm beat," Kristian said with a tired sigh stretching out his arms.

"Me too," Gunny said, exhausted as well.

"Looks like they got us pretty good this time," he said as he looked around surveying the area.

"Yeah, that was a hell of a beating, but on the good side we are still alive," Kristian said with a sly, but reassuring smile. Kristian stood up then reached down to grab Gunny's arm to help lift him to his feet.

"Let's go back and see if there's anything left of our billets," Kristian told Gunny.

"If there's one bunk left I call dibs," Gunny replied, laying claim to the first suitable bunk as his.

"Ok buddy, it's all yours," Kristian said with a smile. Gunny and Kristian walked back to the area where they were billeted.

"Oh, my lord Kristian, look at that. It's amazing. Not a single scratch on the whole building," Gunny said with excitement. The boys looked at each other and smiled then began to sprint toward the door of their billets.

Gunny got to the door first and stopped. "I bet you 5 Marks that I fall asleep faster than you," Gunny said.

"You're on," Kristian said, accepting Gunny's challenge. Gunny excitedly opened the door to the billet and immediately the boys stopped dead in their tracks, amazed. The entire interior of the building was blown completely out of the back side of the building leaving

133

the front of the building untouched as if it was completely intact.

"Have you ever seen anything like this?" Gunny said Kristian.

"No, can't say that I've, but there's a lot of crazy shit that happens during a war," Kristian said. As Kristian and Gunny were talking, a young SS private ran up with some news. The boy was one of the company runners, young boys who can run well and don't tire easily are used to send commands and information from unit to unit. "Units at Mailly, Garney and Coulonges, were all hit. It was like the enemy knew where our units were located," the runner said very excited and still winded from the run.

The young runner sprinted on his way to his next group of comrades that had survived the hellish bombardment, in order to share what little information that he had. Kristian began thinking to himself. (*How would the English know of the locations of each training center for the 12th SS?" It must be some French Resistance spy or maybe… maybe someone in our unit.*)

"No, that's crazy. Everybody knows everybody," Kristian said, convincing himself that it couldn't possibly be an insider, shaking his head and the thought out of his mind. (Hmm,) Kristian began thinking of who could possibly know. (*The only person I told was Holly, but I'm not too worried about her. I wonder if she let something slip out that might have been reported to the French resistance, I will have to remember to ask her about that next time I see her.*)

Kristian began pulling off his field tunic and began to notice that his shirt sleeve was soaked with blood from his shoulder to his hand. "What the hell?" Kristian said as he looked over his arm. "I guess some of that blood out there that I was seeing was my own."

"Well take the rest of your shirt off dumb ass so we can take a look at it," Gunny ordered, with a scowl of disbelief on his face. Kristian pulled off his shirt exposing a wound on his right shoulder and the blood was still slowly coming out. "Oh, that's nothing," Gunny said taking a little tension off of the situation. "Just rub some dirt on it and walk it off, you'll be fine."

Kristian rolled his eyes at Gunny's suggestion and gave him a light shove with his arm. Kristian winced and moaned in pain. "Looks like you're finally feeling the pain after all the adrenalin has gone," Gunny said as he began to wrap the wound on Kristian's shoulder with the non-bled on sleeve of his bloody shirt. "Let's get you over to the medic's station and we will get you sewn up," Gunny ordered, completely taking charge of the situation. As they began walking to the aid station they began to buddy banter with each other.

"You're going to make a hell of a sergeant one day Gunny," Kristian said jokingly.

"Oh no buddy, the first chance I can get the hell out of the military, I'm gone."

"I thought you liked the military Gunny, what changed?" Kristian said.

"I like the uniforms and the friendships. I like shooting guns and blowing things up, but after seeing our guys shot and killed or either blown in half by some

136

bomb, I've got a whole new outlook on things," Gunny said factually.

"What's that?" Kristian said.

"I'm going to keep my head as low to the ground as I can get it and keep my ass alive until I can figure out how to get the hell out of here," Gunny said.

"Don't say that to loud," Kristian told Gunny. "They will stand you up and shoot you for treason."

"Don't worry. Gunny said. It's just between you and me. It…it's our little secret," Gunny said with a wink of his eye.

"I can live with that," Kristian said with a smile. "You know there was a time when I would have turned you in for treason for that." "There was a time when I would have done the same thing, but I think those days are long gone my friend," Gunny said shaking his head with raised eyebrows. "It feels good."

Chapter Thirteen

Around mid-May many flak guns were dispersed

throughout the area in anticipation of an invasion by the Allies.

The area around Dreux and the bridges across the Seine River

were heavily fortified with air defense weapons, as were Elbeuf,

Point-de-l' Arche and Gaillon. The HJ Division were equipped

with the Panther tank. The Panther weighed 45 tons and had a

75-mm gun mounted on the turret, one of the most powerful guns

of the war. The Panther was highly regarded by both Axis and

Allied armies, and was regarded as the best tank developed

during the war.

There was a large surge in equipment and men coming

into the area as Rommel anticipated a beach landing by the

138

American and British armies. The men that were reinforcing Normandy were becoming increasingly hard to come by. The SS itself struggled getting recruits to fill their ranks; public opinion on the SS was changing and not for the better. Many young men wouldn't volunteer for fear of disapproval of their parents and priests as there was now a pronounced anti-SS attitude by the Christian populace.

Recruitment of new SS soldiers was also hampered by the new fear of combat, due to the horror stories that returned home from the battle of Kharkov. Though the Germans eventually took Kharkov, the price that was paid in young men's lives was unacceptable to the German people. Previously there was quite an appeal to join the SS with their Nazi ideology and racial Nordic superiority, but now the changing fortunes in the war were making such considerations appear increasingly hollow.

Kristian and the 12th SS had been training for months in preparation for an Allied invasion that they knew was inevitable. He and his young comrades felt that they were fully prepared for anything the Allies could throw at them, and the majority of them were anxious for the opportunity to prove themselves in battle. The young men had no idea if the invasion would happen tomorrow or a week from tomorrow and the not knowing made the men restless and quite mischievous.

At Kristian's assigned battle position his buddies in his squad began to horseplay and roughly antagonize each other, picking playful fights, working off a little steam. Kristian was quietly sitting by himself watching his friends pitching mock battles with each other with a smile, giggling watching their doltish behavior. "Hey Krissy," one of the boys shouted in an attempt to rile up Kristian so that he would join them. "You too good for us?"

"I'm going to write a letter you idiot," Kristian said. "And to answer your question yes…yes, I'm too good for you,"

Kristian pulled a small pencil and tablet out of the breast pocket of his shirt and leaned back on the stump of a tree that was cut down in order to clear their field of fire. He began to compose a short letter to Holly. Kristian wasn't even sure that he could get a letter to Holly, but if he could, great. If not, it was a good way to kill a little time. It was late in the afternoon and the sun was beginning to go down. Kristian wiggled around trying to get situated to where he was both comfortable and that the sun was shining on his small tablet in order to see what he was writing.

My sweet Holly,

I miss you so much and you are constantly on my mind. Sometimes you are all I can think about, I can't eat and I can't sleep, and all I want is to be next to you. I imagine kissing your lips and touching your soft skin and my heart just aches, almost unbearably. I often daydream about what our lives will be like when the war is over and we can finally be together forever. Together we will be raising our children, creating a family of our own. Sometimes, like now, I've to force myself to stop thinking about you and try to find some other way to occupy my mind, but inevitably you come right back to my mind. Well, enough of that, I don't want to sound too much like a love stricken teenage girl. Not to make you worry, but everyone here is anxiously waiting for the

141

Allies to attack across the channel. We know that there are going to be some decisive battles, but we are all looking forward to it. We hear that the Allies call us "The baby milk division," but we are not afraid and we will show them that we are no babies. We have had intense training with our weapons and I'm sure we can handle anything the can throw at us. They tell us that the enemy is physically superior to us, but we are quick, agile and very confident. Our officers and non-coms have been hardened by battle on the Eastern Front and we have known them since the beginning of training. During combat training with live ammunition they were down in the mud with us, in steel helmets and submachine-guns. The Allied bomber squadrons drone overhead day after day, and we are constantly fearing that they will drop their loads on us, but our confidence remains high. Enough of the gloom and doom, I just want you to know that I love you and cannot wait to see our baby. Hopefully we will be able to defeat the Allies quickly and I'll soon be able to see you again. Please write me soon and tell me all about wonderful things

that are going on in your life that are absolutely nothing

about the war.

My love forever,

Kristian

After Kristian had finished his letter, he kissed the paper, carefully folded it and placed it in his breast pocket for safe keeping.

"I bet I know who you were writing," Gunny said as he walked up behind Kristian.

"Hey my friend, where have you been?" Kristian said with a smile glad to see Gunny.

"I got detailed out to help build barbed wire barricades for the roads so we can use them as road blocks," Gunny explained. "We will be checking identification of everyone using the road, so you know what that means,"

"Yes," Kristian said with a disgruntled groan. "Guard duty."

"Yes, my friend, guard duty," Gunny said with a grin. "And guess what, you have to pull duty at 6 a.m."

"Oh great," Kristian said sarcastically. "Well, I better get some good rest tonight if I'm going to be on my feet all day tomorrow."

"Well, this might make you feel a little better," Gunny said factually. "I not only built those damn barricades, but I get to pull guard duty in front of them with you all day tomorrow." Kristian gave Gunny a big smile with a hint of gratification. "Yeah, I thought that might make you happy," Gunny said as he kicked Kristian in the leg with a snarly look on his face.

At 6 a.m. Kristian and Gunny reported for guard duty at the road barricade and were briefed by the sergeant on duty of their rolls at the checkpoint. The sergeant was about 6'5'', a huge beast of a man with a scar that ran down the left side of his face as if sliced open by a bayonet or sword in brutal hand to hand combat. Just the site of the man struck fear in both Kristian and Gunny. They both found it hard to concentrate on what the sergeant was telling them due to their thoughts of what that man

144

could possibly do to them if he had the desire to. Kristian's duty was to check the identification papers of all who passed their checkpoint and Gunny's duties were to move the barricade out of the way so those who were allowed to pass had an unobstructed right-of-way.

"I want you idiots to make damn sure everyone has the proper paperwork before you allow them to pass," the sergeant said with a growl. "I find out you screw up and I'll have your asses, you boys got it?" Both Kristian and Gunny snapped to attention. "Yes sergeant," they said in unison, eyes open wide in fear of their mortality. The duty sergeant walked away and the boys looked at each other, eyes still wide open in shock.

"Holy crap," Gunny said just a tad bit frazzled. "That guy is one mean son of a bitch."

"Yeah," Kristian said. "He looks like he could gut you like a fish, then lick the blade of the knife clean."

"No shit," Gunny said. "I'm going to make damn sure that I don't piss that guy off."

"I'm with you buddy," Kristian said with a fearful look on his face and an agreeing nod of his head. "Well, let's get started." The boys took their positions, Kristian standing at the side of the road and Gunny by the barricade ready to move it at a moment's notice.

The boys stood there, just staring at each other with nothing to do but wait for someone to come and request to pass. After an hour and a half of just staring at each other, Gunny found the boredom unbearable and had to do something. He looked at his watch to see how much longer they had to stand guard before they were relieved. "Only six and a half hours to go," Gunny said with a heavy and exhausted sigh.

"Oh crap," Kristian replied, dropping his head to his chest in anguish. Just as the boys began to wallow in their misery the sound of a bicycle bell in the distance gratefully grabbed their attention.

With truly excited anticipation the boys turned their heads in the direction of the sound's welcomed interruption. They both strained to see who was coming down the road but all they could make out was an undefinable silhouette on a bicycle

146

in the distance. As the rider came closer the boys could see that the cyclist was a female in her early twenties. "Hey Krissy, look at that," Gunny said with a cat that ate the canary smile. Kristian smiled back at Gunny and shook his head. The young woman rode her bike up to the barricade and stopped, smiling at the boys as if she was just as happy to see them as they were to see her.

"Papers please," Kristian requested, holding out his hand for her to give him her identification. He began to look at her papers and everything seemed to be in order. Kristian looked up from the young woman's identification papers and glanced at Gunny, making sure that he was at his proper position and ready to move the barricade. Gunny had a smile on his face that made him look somewhere between a lunatic and an idiot, chomping at the bit for an opportunity to talk to this girl. "Gerta Dupree?" Kristian said curiously. "A French surname and a German given name. That is rather odd, how did that come to be?"

"My grandmother was German and I was named after her, and thanks to my parents, I've been catching hell for it my whole life,"

Kristian smiled at Greta and chuckled. "I can see how that might be a problem since Germany and France has had two wars in thirty years."

"Yes, exactly," Greta said with a smile. As Kristian and Greta chuckled about the oddity, Kristian glanced back over to Gunny.

Gunny still had that idiotic smile on his face and it was almost to the point of being creepy. "Hey, lover boy," Kristian said to Gunny as he snapped his fingers next to Gunny's face. "Just say hello."

"Uh… hello," Gunny said, verbally tripping over himself. Kristian and Greta looked at each other and smiled, then Greta tuned back to Gunny.

"Hello," Greta said with a smile that radiated both empathy and sympathy.

"Okay Gunny, her papers are in order, let her pass." Gunny pulled the barricade out of the way so that Greta could pass, the whole time staring at Greta with that silly smile on his face. Greta, both flattered and embarrassed, shyly smiled and peddled her bicycle past Gunny and the barricade as she continued on her way.

"Hey Gunny, if she looks back at you she likes you," Kristian said with a grin. "God would only know why though."

Gunny and Kristian both watched Greta ride away, eagerly wanting to see her turn to look back. "Come on, come on, turn around," Gunny said as if trying to mentally will her to look back at him. Trying not to let the boys see her, Greta turned to take a quick glance back at Gunny. "Woo hoo," Gunny said as he jumped up and down, arms raised in victory with a smile from ear to ear. "She looked," Gunny said excitedly as he did a silly dance.

"Yeah she did buddy, she sure did," Kristian said with a smile as he patted his giddy friend on his shoulder.

Chapter Fourteen

As the day passed, in between the occasional civilian or military personnel that passed through their checkpoint, Kristian and Gunny killed time watching the French citizens who were working for the Germans to build fortifications. The French workers moved around freely with little to no supervision, leaving the doors wide open for espionage. "Don't you think that is strange?" Kristian said Gunny.

"What?" Gunny said. "There are no guards watching the French workers. What if one of them were part of the French underground? They would know every position that we have," Kristian said, sincerely concerned about the situation.

150

"Relax," Gunny said in an attempt to reassure Kristian. "I'm sure they thoroughly check out each one of those workers before they're allowed to work for us."

"I sure hope so," Kristian said. "It sure leaves me with an uneasy feeling though, I mean, you never know. One of them could be a spy."

"Pfff, not likely," Gunny said with a look on his face like Kristian was an idiot. "They probably have the Gestapo look at the background of each one of them, and you couldn't hide a fart you let ten years ago from those guys." "Yeah, I guess you're right," Kristian said a little more reassured. "Hey, snap to, there's a truck coming,"

A beat-up Opel Blitz, a German three-ton supply truck that looked like it had been to hell and back pulled up to the barricade and came to a quick stop just feet away from where Gunny was standing. Angry that the truck had almost hit him, Gunny hit the hood of the truck with his hand. "Hey asshole, you almost hit me."

The young private that could have barely been all of sixteen stuck his head out of the truck window.

"I'm sorry, the brakes on this beat up peace of shit don't work worth crap."

Gunny stood there in front of the truck shaking his head and rolling his eyes in disbelief. "Papers please," Kristian requested from the young private.

The young boy reached into his breast pocket and pulled out his identification then handed it to Kristian. Kristian looked over the boy's papers, "where are you headed Private…Houst?" Kristian asked.

"I'm heading to Falaise," the private said. "I deliver supplies there every couple of days." Kristian's eyes opened wide, and an excited and joyful smile came over his face from an epiphany that had just filled his head.

"Hey, could you deliver a letter to my girl in Falaise for me?" Kristian asked the private.

"Sure, you bet," the young private said. "I don't have much else to do when I get there and who knows, she just might have a friend for me,"

"Wonderful, that's the attitude," Kristian said.

"Thank you. Her name is Holly; I'll write her address on the back of the letter for you. Tell her that I love and miss her and that I'll come to see her as soon as I can."

"I'll do," the private said. "And thank you, I just might get me a little French girl to play with," The Private said with a smile on his face as he wiggled around in his seat with excitement. Kristian handed the letter to the private and nodded at Gunny to move the barricade so that the truck could pass.

"Okay, private move out," Kristian told the boy waving him on to pass. "Be careful and keep that truck on the road," Kristian shouted to the driver as he pulled away. "I need that letter to get there." The driver gave a quick look with a smile and a wave to Kristian as he continued to drive away from the checkpoint and on to his destination. "Isn't that wonderful?" Kristian said to Gunny excitedly. "I figured out how to get a letter to Holly."

"Well, I don't think it's that wonderful," Gunny said with a frown.

"Why is that?" Kristian said both surprised and curious at Gunny's reply.

"Because Holly may introduce the girl that she was supposed to introduce to me, to that little runt,"

"Don't worry Gunny," Kristian said reassuring his love starved comrade. "I'm sure that she has more than one friend."

About two hundred meters away a type 166 Schwimmwagen, the German version of the American Jeep, was coming toward Kristian's checkpoint. The Schwimmwagen, unlike the American Jeep, had one extra remarkable feature. The car was designed not only as a cross-country vehicle, but it also had amphibious capabilities that allowed it to float and traverse waterways. As the vehicle came closer to the checkpoint, the driver's side front tire of the vehicle had a blow out and the car began to violently swerve back and forth across the road until the driver regained control and was able to come to a complete stop on the side of the road.

154

The Schwimmwagen, though loved by German command staff, had no doors, so to get in or out of the car one had to physically crawl over the side of the vehicle. This, at times, was found to be rather difficult for senior officers due to their physical limitations. Regardless of the physical challenges, many officers willingly made the sacrifice of convenience for the love of the car. The driver quickly sprang out of the car to assess the damage to the tire and discovered that it was clearly evident the tire had to be changed.

Kristian and Gunny could see three officers crawl out of the Schwimmwagen and they began to walk toward the checkpoint. As the three officers came closer they recognized German General Chief of Staff of VIII Corps Erich Marcks and two other officers that they did not recognize. General Marcks had authored the first draft of the operational plan, *Operation Draft East*, for Operation Barbarossa, the invasion of the Soviet Union and had lost a leg during combat on the Eastern Front. General Marcks had won the medal of The Knight's Cross of the Iron Cross with Oak Leaves and was considered a great hero of Germany and the Third Reich.

155

Kristian and Gunny looked at each other with both disbelief and excitement in getting the opportunity to personally see this great German warrior and the thought of them to actually get to meet the General in person was almost unfathomable. The three officers stopped walking about twenty meters from the barricade and began talking about preparations for the Allied invasion. "I see "Rommel's Asparagus" is coming along well," one of them said pointing out to the field on each side of the road. "Rommel's Asparagus" was 13-to-16-foot (4 to 5 m) logs which the Axis placed in the fields and meadows of Normandy to cause damage and death to the men in the expected invasion of Allied military gliders.

"I expect the Allied invasion to come in June," the General told the other officers. "I also expect the first landing to be successful. I'm not sure that we will be able to drive back the enemy with the forces that I currently have. We are absolutely dependent on the provision of additional forces and I expect that the HJ Division will be assigned to me, increasing the chance of pushing the Allies back into the sea." "It is absolutely crucial that the division is allocated to me for the defense of the coast."

"Yes sir," the two junior officers said to Marcks, following close behind as the General continued to walk toward the barricade.

When the General reached the barricade, Kristian and Gunny snapped their boot heels and stood sharply at attention, their hearts pounding with excitement. Then, in unison, raised their arms in the traditional Nazi salute shouting, "Heil Hitler." General Marcks barely raised his arm to return the salute and with very little enthusiasm replied, "Heil Hitler." The boys slowly lowered their arms, both feeling slightly disappointed with the General is response to their salute. Without a word, the General began looking over the boys, inspecting their uniforms and the shine on their boots.

"Fine, fine," the general said to the boys. "You young men look very squared away. You know you two represent the entire Third Reich. How the French see you is how they will see the entire Reich. You represent not only the HJ Division, but all of Germany."

"Yes sir," the boys said.

"Are you boys ready to fight?" The general said raising his head, looking down his nose as if he knew what they boys were expected to say.

"Yes sir."

"Very good then," the general told the boys. "Carry on with your duties men."

"Yes sir," the boys replied.

The general and the two accompanying officers began to slowly walk back to the command car as the driver was finished replacing the tire on the vehicle. As they walked, the general continued informing the two officers of his directives for the HJ Division that were to be carried out in preparation of the Allied landing. "I want men deployed on each crossing of the Seine between Paris and Rouen," the general ordered. "I also want deployment between the mouths of the Seine and Orne rivers as well as men prepared for action northwest and west of Caen."

"Yes sir," the junior officers said to the General.

"Well, I guess we know what's coming down the road," Kristian told Gunny.

"What, the general?"

"No dummy, the orders to move out to guard the river crossings and when they expect the Allies to attack," Kristian said.

"Oh, yeah," Gunny said with a smile, shaking his head. "I guess we know more about what's going to happen even before our commander does." "You better keep quiet about it though, you don't want to chance getting our butts in a sling," Kristian said earnestly.

"Don't worry buddy, I know how to keep my mouth shut," Gunny said. "It is kind of fun though knowing more than anyone else does."

Gunny opened the barricade for General Marcks command vehicle to pass then Kristian and Gunny gave the general one last respectful salute as the General passed by. The general returned the salute with a smile of approval of the boys as if wishing them luck and the boys watched the general's car as it drove out of sight. "Wow, I still can't believe we met General Marcks, no one will believe us," Gunny said.

"It doesn't matter if they do or don't, we will always know," Kristian said. The next hour was uneventful until a column of Panzer V Panther tanks on their way to Caen rumbled down the road from the north to the checkpoint.

Kristian and Gunny watched the tanks as they lumbered down the road toward the checkpoint. Suddenly the column abruptly stopped and the crews began jumping out of the tanks, running across the road and diving into the ditches that ran parallel to the road. The tank crews quickly bailed out of their tanks and jumped into a ditch seemingly out of the blue until the second tank in the column exploded from a five-inch rocket fired from an American P-47 Thunderbolt fighter bomber.

The aircraft also opened up with its 8 x 0.5 Browning machine-guns, strafing everything in its path and ripping apart the bodies of men that had the misfortune of not clearing the column fast enough to escape the overwhelming firepower of the deadly aircraft. Kristian and Gunny quickly took cover in the ditch beside the checkpoint hoping they were far enough away from the column that they themselves would not be in danger. Seconds after the first attacking aircraft passed over, a second Thunderbolt dropped two canisters of napalm directly on the ditch where the tank crews were attempting to conceal themselves from the carnage.

As quickly as the attack began it ended. The devastation the allied attack had inflicted upon the column of Panzers was horrifying. Ninety percent of the tank crews were instantly incinerated when the Thunderbolt dropped the napalm on the ditch that they were taking cover in. Five percent of the crews were killed by the Browning machine-gun fire with only one Panzer tank destroyed. Kristian and Gunny crawled out of the ditch and began to walk toward the column in a state of shock trying to comprehend what had just taken place.

Bodies of men were burning alongside of the road. Morbidly charred, some with mouths open as if screaming and others with outstretched arms as if reaching for someone to save them. The sight of this was too much for Gunny; he fell to his knees and began to throw up uncontrollably. Kristian kneeled down beside Gunny and put his hand on Gunny's shoulder in an effort to comfort his friend and ease his distress. "Come on buddy," Kristian told Gunny. "You have to get it together, we have to help the wounded," Gunny wiped his mouth with the sleeve of his shirt and slowly got to his feet. "Are you ok now?" Kristian said sympathetically.

"Yeah, yeah, I'm good," Gunny said. "Ok, let's go see if we can help anyone."

Chapter Fifteen

After a horrific day, Kristian climbed into his bunk to bed down for the evening. Exhausted, he quickly fell into a deep sleep and began to dream. of his peaceful youth, surrounded by warmth and love at his childhood home. It was a beautiful spring day, and he could hear birds singing, flying from tree to tree high above the fields of wildflowers. Kristian sat at the kitchen table, the smell of fresh cookies that his mother was baking filled the air with a comforting aroma. Walking toward Kristian, his mother held out a plate of the freshly baked cookies with a loving smile on her heart soothing face.

Kristian smiled as he looked into his mother's aging blue eyes and reached for one of the fresh cookies his mother had just

163

lovingly baked. Suddenly, Kristian's mother let out a blood curdling scream as flames began to engulf her, burning his mother alive. As his mother's body charred black as coal from the flames, she began to look like one of the bodies of the burned soldiers he had seen earlier in the day. Her arms stretched out as if trying to reach Kristian to save herself. Her mouth opened, blustering a spine-chilling scream as her body was slowly consumed by the flames. Kristian woke from his nightmare with a whimpered scream, eyes wide open in shock at the horror he had just beheld. He quickly sat straight up in his bunk, panting heavily trying to catch his breath, his body covered in a cold sweat.

"Hey buddy, are you okay?" Gunny asked, concerned, looking up from the letter he had been writing. There was no reply from Kristian, he just continued to pant and look as if he had seen some blood-curdling vision. "Kristian…hey snap out of it, are you okay?" Gunny said again.

"Yes," Kristian replied, almost in a whisper quickly shaking his head yes.

"Did you have a bad dream?" Gunny said.

"What do you think dumb ass?" Kristian said angrily still panting.

"Sorry I asked," Gunny said as he went back to writing his letter.

"I'm sorry, I shouldn't take it out on you," Kristian apologized. "I just had a really bad dream."

"It's okay," Gunny said. "Anything you want to talk about?"

"No…no, I'll be okay," Kristian said as he cupped his face with his hands rubbing his eyes, then running his fingers through his hair ending with a quick scratch of his head. "Just a really bad dream about my mom."

"I have dreams like that sometimes," Gunny said, trying to reassure Kristian that he was not alone experiencing these nightmares. "One time I had a dream that some Russians caught my little sister. They began to break her arms and legs with a metal rod; she screamed and screamed until she finally passed out. The Russians stopped beating her when she blacked out then were kind enough to wait for her to regain consciousness before they threw her off of a roof of an apartment building. It was horrible. I couldn't get a good night's sleep for about a week after that. It really screwed with my head."

"Thanks for being empathic Gunny, but that really doesn't help," Kristian said with a hint of a stink face.

"Sorry buddy, just wanted you to know that you're not alone and that I have them too," Gunny said with a look of sincerity on his young face. Kristian looked down at the ground shaking his head yet letting Gunny know that he understood his intentions.

"Come on, let's try and get us some sleep," Gunny said. "Dream about that little French girl of yours."

Kristian's face lit up with an elated smile at the thought of Holly. Seeing Kristian's face, Gunny returned the smile and they both laid back on their pillows, their eyes staring up at the ceiling. "Lights out," the duty sergeant yelled into the billets, and the room went dark.

The next morning before wakeup call, Kristian awoke to the smell of breakfast cooking at the field kitchen. This morning Kristian was a bit hungrier than normal, so he carefully and quietly put his uniform on as to not wake the other men and headed out of the billets. Kristian wanted to get to the kitchen before the other soldiers in order to be one of the first of the men to get a meal. Sometimes the wait in line could be from twenty to thirty minutes and Kristian was so hungry that he didn't want to wait that long. The smell of the food drifting in from the open windows of the billets increased Kristian's hunger to the point that he had to hold his stomach in pain with his hand as it angrily growled like an animal to be fed.

German soldiers at the front were served food prepared by a horse drawn field kitchen that could cook enough stew for a company of men as well as hundreds of loaves of bread a day. The kitchen was often nicknamed the "field cannon" because of the bellowing thick black smoke that came out of the smoke stack. Unlike other armies the German combat soldiers received first priority for food rations. There were rear echelon men who volunteered for combat just for the opportunity to get better food due to the sacrifices being made in the rear to support the men at the front. Breakfast typically consisted of 2 slices of bread with jam or some fatty meat mixed with onions as well as one cup of ersatz coffee, usually made from chicory nuts or acorns or whatever nut were available in the area to be ground up and boiled.

Kristian was sitting, leaning against an old oak tree eating the last piece of his jam covered bread when Eric, one of the new replacements, ran up to Kristian and kneeled down beside him. "Hey Kristian," the young boy said panting heavily from his run to find him.

"There's a French man… and a woman… asking for you at the checkpoint on the road."

"Did they tell you what they wanted?" Kristian said.

"Yes," Eric said. "They wanted you."

Kristian gave Eric a roll of his eyes insinuating that the young man was an idiot. "Did they tell you their names?" Kristian asked with a snarly frown.

"No, they just asked for you," Eric said with a sarcastic smile.

Kristian stood up and headed to the checkpoint with pep in his step, very curious who would be asking to see him. As Kristian drew closer to the checkpoint he could just make out a girl's silhouette standing up waving at him from an old red 1925 Delage Torpedo convertible.

"Kristian," the girl shouted as she waved.

Kristian knew immediately that it was Holly's sweet loving voice and a smile came over Kristian's face from ear to ear. Kristian ran over to the passenger's side of the car and met Holly with a hug as she came out of the car door, picking her up off of the ground and spinning around with her as if they were dancing.

"What are you doing here?" Kristian asked, not really caring why, just ecstatic to see her.

"A truck driver, a Private Houst dropped off your letter and told me where you were, so here I am," Holly said with a smile and a quick peck on Kristian's cheek. Holly looked over to the man that was driving the car. "You remember my cousin Henry, don't you?"

"Oh yes," Kristian said. "I remember Henry. How are you? It's nice to see you again," Kristian said with a smile, extending his hand to shake Henry's. Henry kept his hands on the steering wheel and with a slight snarl on his face nodded his head acknowledging Kristian. Kristian dropped his hand and looked at Holly. "I see he still has that sparkling personality," Kristian said sarcastically.

"Oh, don't mind him," Holly said. "He just has to get to know you. He'll warm up to you, you'll see."

"Hey, let's get some pictures of us while I'm here," Holly said excitedly. "I brought a camera and this way I can see your handsome face all the time and I'll send you copies so you'll have pictures of us as well."

"That sounds like a great idea," Kristian said, more than willing to get some photos of him and such a beautiful girl together that he could show off to his comrades. "Henry, you take some photos of us with the camera," Holly told Henry as she handed him the camera. "What are all of those poles sticking up out in the field?" Holly said pointing at the odd sight.

"Those are what we call Rommel's Asparagus," Kristian said almost boasting. They're to snag and destroy allied gliders if they try to land here."

"Oh, how fascinating," Holly said. "Let's get one of us with those in the background."

Kristian stood tall, proud as a peacock next to Holly with his arm around the back side of her waist as Henry took a photo of them with Rommel's little surprise in the background.

"Fantastic, that will be a good one," Holly said to Kristian. "Hey, let's get one with all of those tanks in the background, that would be a good one too." Kristian eagerly complied with Holly's request without hesitation. "What are those big guns over there?" Holly asked, pointing at a Flak 18 and 36 anti-aircraft guns accompanied with a Flak 43 anti-aircraft gun.

"Those my dear are for shooting down those damn allied aircraft that continually harass us," Kristian said.

"Ooh, let's get some pictures with those as well," Holly said. "All the girls will be jealous when they see these."

Henry continued to shoot photos of Kristian and Holly all around the area that wasn't restricted until they had run out of film. "Holly, I would love to stay and spend more time with you, but I have ammo detail today and I'm late reporting for duty, so I unfortunately have to go," Kristian said with regret on his face. "I may be in a little trouble, but I don't want to get in so much trouble that I can't get a pass this weekend. That would mean I couldn't come to see you, and I definitely don't want that to happen."

"I understand," Holly said. "I don't want you to get in trouble."

Kristian walked Holly over to the car and opened the door for her to climb in. He closed the car door as Holly sat

172

down in her seat, then Kristian leaned down and gave Holly a gentle loving kiss.

Holly cupped her hand on Kristian's cheek. "I'll be waiting for you," Holly said in almost a whisper, then kissed Kristian one last time with enough passion that it would ensure that Kristian would make every effort possible to be there with her. Kristian stepped back away from the car and watched as Henry turned the car around on the road, Kristian's and Holly's eyes never leaving each other as the car turned away and drove out of site. The two young guards that were posted at the checkpoint walked up from behind and stood next to Kristian also watching the car drive out of site. "You are a lucky man," one of the guards told Kristian shamelessly envious of him.

"Yes, my friend, yes, I am," Kristian said with a smile, then quietly and slowly walked away to report for duty.

Chapter Sixteen

A couple of uneventful days had passed, filled with dirty, sweaty work digging trenches and building gun emplacement platforms for the anti-aircraft batteries. This was just time-consuming work that officers of every army give their enlisted men to do in order to keep the men from shooting each other out of sheer boredom. Just before nightfall, Kristian and the rest of his exhausted platoon staggered into the barracks. Each of the men collapsing on their individual bunks. "This is bullshit," Gunny grunted as he and Kristian fell backwards onto their bunks. "I'm a soldier, not a plumber," Gunny complained.

"The life of a soldier isn't all daisies and rainbows," Kristian said to Gunny. "You knew that when you joined."

Gunny didn't reply to Kristian's remark, he needed no word to explain the "go to hell" look on his face. Kristian smiled and the boys both laid their heads back on their pillows to rest.

"Ackmann," a shout by a young voice came from the entrance to the billets. "Is there a Kristian Ackmann in here?"

"I'm Ackmann," Kristian said, jumping up from his bunk waving his arm in an attempt to get the boys attention.

"Letter for you," the boy said holding out his arm, letter in hand as he walked to where Kristian was standing. A smile came over Kristian's face as he took the letter from the boy's hand. "Who's it from?" Kristian asked.

"I don't know," the boy said. "I don't read other people's mail."

Kristian began to open the envelope but discovered that it had already been opened. "Hey," Kristian said, upset at what he was seeing. "Someone already opened the letter."

175

Kristian and the boys from his platoon that had been gathering around to hear what was in the letter looked at the boy that delivered the letter both questionable and accusingly. The boy looked around at all of the faces that were staring at him and a look of fear, as if he had been discovered, came over his face. The boy quickly turned and ran out of the billets as fast as his young feet could carry him. The boys in the platoon began looking around at each other, laughing at the fleeing boy.

Kristian pulled out the letter from the envelope.

"Ah, it's from Holly," Kristian said, then sat down on his bunk and began quietly reading the letter.

"Hey, asshole, read it out loud," one of the boys shouted.

"This is private stuff between me and my girl," Kristian said. "If you want a little romance you are going to have to find your own girl."

"Some of us aren't quite as lucky as you are, Krissy, and we have to live precariously through you," a boy shouted.

"Yeah, that's right," another boy said in agreement, then turned to the boy standing next to him and almost in a whisper said. "Hey, what does precariously mean?"

"That means he better read it, or we are going to beat the crap out of him," the boy next to him explained. "Yeah, precariously," the clearly illiterate boy spouted with a firm look of conviction.

Kristian rolled his eyes. "Okay, okay I'll read you the letter, but if it starts getting personal you guys will just have to move on, because I'm not sharing any of that with you." In unison there was a moan of disappointment from the boys gathered around that were anticipating hearing some juicy tidbits that they might be able to dream about that night. Kristian unfolded the letter, gave a quick look at all of the faces around him shining with a look of pure anticipation, and began to read.

Dear Krissy,

I hope you are doing well. I miss you very much and I constantly think about the next time we are together.

Hearing this the guys started giggling and nudging each other in the ribs with their elbows. "Knock it off you idiots, and get your minds out of the gutter," Kristian said, scolding the boys. "Holly's a good girl."

"That's not what I hear. From what I hear there's not one good girl in France," one of the boys said loudly followed by a group chuckle.

"Alright you idiots, that's it. No more letter for you," Kristian said with a hint of anger and frustration with the other boys in his voice. Again, the boys moaned in disappointment. The loud sound of an air raid siren suddenly filled the air and the lights inside the billets went out, along with all other lights in the surrounding area.

The boys rushed around in the semi-darkness gathering their gear and weapons and immediately sprinted out of the billets to their duty stations. In the night sky the droning of the engines from the approaching British Lancaster Bombers drew ever closer minute by minute. Every man knew what was to come and each in their own way tried to make peace with God, there are no atheists in foxholes. As the sound of the aircraft came nearly overhead, spotlights began lighting up the sky, searching for enemy aircraft. Flak 41 Anti-Aircraft Cannons followed suit in an attempt to get a clear shot at any prey that were unfortunate enough to be exposed by the powerful lights. The telltale whistling sounds made by the bombs being dropped from the bellies of the British planes began to fill the air from what seemed to be everywhere.

Kristian and Gunny squatted down in the bottom of the foxhole trying to make their bodies as small a target as possible. The bombs dropped from the aircraft began hitting the ground, and the ferocity of the explosions was utterly terrifying. The boys could hear the bombs dropping closer and closer, as if they were steps of a mountainous demon from hell coming for their souls. Kristian cupped his hands over his ears and began to scream in an attempted battle cry of bravery, but to no avail. His scream clearly expressed unbridled fear and he began to cry uncontrollably like a frightened child in the dark. The experience reminded Kristian of the horror he had experienced in one of the night bombing raids back in Berlin. The death, destruction and

179

pure terror were something that he, no matter how he tried, could never forget.

The explosions drew ever closer and the boys prepared themselves for their inevitable demise; they were sure they were not going to get out of this one alive. One of the allied bombs exploded just meters away, throwing a large amount of dirt and debris into the air. The dirt falling back to the ground nearly filled the foxhole Kristian and Gunny were in, burying the boys alive. Kristian began to wiggle and claw his way out of the dirt to free himself. The effort was exhausting, and the lack of air to breath began to take its toll on Kristian. The more he struggled the weaker he became, but just before Kristian reached the point of blacking out he reached the top, freeing himself from his potential grave.

Kristian gasped for air, sucking in deep breaths in an effort to bring himself back into full consciousness and out of the grasp of death. As the bombs continued to drop, their detonations became further and further away. Kristian regained his composure and began to look around for Gunny, but he was nowhere in sight. "Gunny," Kristian shouted frantically. There was no doubt in Kristian's mind where Gunny was, still buried in the dirt. He desperately began digging where Gunny had been sitting, calling out his friend's name repeatedly as he dug like a dog with his bare hands. Kristian was determined that he was not going to let his buddy die, by being buried alive. If he had to die he would die like a soldier, honorably, a warrior in combat.

Kristian continued to dig and about a meter below the top of the soil, Kristian felt the top of Gunny's steel helmet. Kristian used his hands to dig around the sides of Gunny's helmet, trying to free his face from the surrounding dirt. Kristian felt the visor on the front of Gunny's helmet giving Kristian confirmation of the location of Gunny's face. He began pulling the dirt away from his young comrade's face in an effort to allow him to breathe, but Gunny's lungs made no effort to draw any air. Kristian quickly continued to dig to the point where he could pull Gunny's lifeless body from the engulfing dirt. In the 1940's CPR hadn't been created yet, so Kristian laid Gunny on his back and straddled his body and lifted him by pulling him up by his belt then lowering him back to the ground repeatedly in an effort to revive him.

Surprisingly, after a few dozen repetitions of this primitive revival method, Gunny began to gasp for his first breaths of air. He collapsed, falling to the ground lying beside his buddy, drained and panting from the struggle. "Oh boy, I thought you were a goner," Kristian told Gunny.

"I saw Jesus," Gunny said.

"What?" Kristian said bewildered at what Gunny had just confessed.

"I saw Jesus, he is for real," Gunny said with conviction.

"Have you lost your mind, Jesus?" Kristian said.

"Yes," Gunny said.

"Well, what did good old Jesus say?" Kristian said with a hint of sarcasm.

"He just smiled at me and told me that I wasn't done and that I had more to do. Then he said that I've to go back, but I didn't want to go. It felt wonderful there, peaceful and love."

"Love?" Kristian said confused about what Gunny was sharing with him.

182

"Yes, I can't explain it. It was just an overwhelming feeling of love."

"Well, tell Jesus to stick around we may need him," Kristian said with a chuckle.

"You laugh, but I was there. He was for real," Gunny said without any reservation.

"I never knew you were the religious type," Kristian said.

"I wasn't, I never believed in God or Jesus. I just thought it was all just crazy superstition," Gunny said also surprised by revelation.

"How do you know it was Jesus, did he say he was Jesus?" Kristian said, now getting more curious about the experience his friend had just had.

"No, he didn't say he was Jesus, I just knew somehow. It was like he didn't have to say it, it was known. I can't explain it, it was like a feeling or like I was told in my head or something, but I know it was real," Gunny tried to explain.

"Well, you have never given me a reason to doubt you, I won't start now. I guess if you're going to meet Jesus or the Devil, you got the better of the two, you must be doing something right," Kristian said with a smile and a pat on Gunny's shoulder.

The air raid siren sounded again as the lights that were still working in the area came on giving an all clear to the battered troops that survived the allied onslaught. "Well, are you okay now?" Kristian said with concern. "Yes, I'm okay," Gunny said.

"Do you feel up to giving a hand to the guys that are injured, or do you need to rest a while?" Kristian said.

"I'm ok, I'm ok. Why do the *Tommies* (The Germans nickname for the British) always hit us at night, don't they know we need our sleep?" Gunny said jokingly.

"Maybe their women don't give them anything to do at night, so they try to keep us up all night too," Kristian said returning the jest.

The boys both chuckled at themselves for their levity. "Alright," Kristian said with a light slap to Gunny's helmet, "let's go see who needs help."

Chapter Seventeen

On Saturday Kristian was allowed an overnight leave

pass and caught a ride with Private Houst, the young supply

truck driver, that relayed letters between Kristian and Holly.

Kristian was lucky enough to unexpectedly get a pass, but he had

no time to relay a message to Holly in order to inform her that he

had the opportunity to come see her in Falaise, and had no idea if

she would be there or not. The old supply truck they were riding

in rattled and the worn engine moaned as it struggled down the

road. "Damn Houst, this crappy old thing going to make it to

Falaise?" Kristian ask concerned with a hint of sarcasm in his

voice.

"Hey, she's not crappy. This old girl may be a little battered, but she has never failed me yet."

"Ok," Kristian said with a smile. "Hey Houst, what is your fist name anyway?"

"Decker... Decker Houst," he said.

"Decker, that's a good name, I like it," Kristian said nodding his head in approval.

"Yeah, it means man of prayer," he said proudly.

"Are you religious?" Kristian said a little surprised at what Decker had just told him.

"Sort of I guess," Decker said. "I mean, I'm a Christian if that's what you're asking."

"Wow, that's kind of strange," Kristian said with a puzzled look on his face.

"What's that?" Decker said.

"Just the other day a buddy of mine told me that he met Jesus," Kristian said.

"Wow, can't say I've ever done that," Decker said wide-eyed.

"What a strange coincidence, its twice in a week I heard of Jesus," Kristian said a little baffled.

"Well, maybe it's the old man upstairs way of telling you that you need to get good with God," Decker said.

"Maybe it's a nudge in the ribs; you know they expect the Allies to hit the beaches any day now and no one lives forever."

Kristian sat in the truck silently contemplating the strange coincidence for a moment then leaned his head on the back of the seat. The rocking of the truck as it rolled down the road and light rumble of the engine quickly made Kristian doze off. He had just completed a fun filled week of digging trenches and filling bomb craters with dirt to level out the land around the camp ground where his unit was stationed. Decker glanced over at Kristian and smiled at Kristian's head rocking back and forth as he slept traveling down the road. There had been many times that he had felt like doing the same while taking this route to Falaise, but unfortunately was not able to due to both being the one in control of the vehicle and the lack of wanting to die in a fiery crash.

"Hey sleepyhead, we're here," Decker said shaking Kristian's leg. Kristian groggily awoke with a yawn and a stretch of his arms. "You were absolutely no company at all," Decker complained. "You owe me pal."

"Okay," Kristian said within another yawn. "What do you want?"

"I want you to have Holly introduce me to one of her friends."

"Well, I can ask, but I can't make any guarantees," Kristian said.

"I'm sure she knows some girl that would like to meet me, girls always have lots of other girlfriends. Besides, I would be a great catch," Decker boasted proudly with a matter of fact look on his face.

"We will let her have a look at you and she can determine which of her girlfriends with low self-esteem might be desperate enough to go out with a scrawny kid like you," Kristian said taunting Decker.

189

"Hey, that's not a real smart thing to say for a guy who is going to need a ride back to camp tomorrow," Decker said with a raised brow.

"How long do we have to wait around here before we can head over to Holly's house?" Kristian asked.

"All I've to do is report in that the delivery is here, wait for the privates to unload the truck and then have the sergeant sign off on the proof of delivery paperwork and we can slip out of here for the rest of the day. I've got a great job," Decker said with a smile, nodding his head for his good fortune.

"I can say it beats the hell out of digging trenches like I've been doing all week," Kristian said with a snarl.

Decker chuckled at Kristian's misery. "You just hang around a little while, but stay out of the way; a lot of trucks come in and out of here and some of those idiots drive like lunatics."

190

"Thanks for the heads up," Kristian said as opened the door of the truck, pondering what he could do to kill a little time.

Kristian paced around near the trucks, occasionally giving a rock a kick as he thought about Holly, imagining in his head how it would be to see her again and what they might do with their time together. Kristian's anticipation was driving him nuts and he began to grow a little impatient waiting on Decker, beginning to get a little angry it was taking so long to get the truck unloaded.

"Hey," Decker said coming running up from behind Kristian.

Kristian quickly spun around and a smile of relief replaced the frustration he had been feeling waiting on Decker. "Finally," Kristian said, happy Decker had finally showed up so they could go to Holly's house.

"Relax, sometimes it takes a little time to get those lazy bastards off of their asses to do their job," Decker explained. "Let's go see your girl."

The boys walked down the road in a quick step headed for the town. It was a short walk to Holly's house and as they walked Kristian began to wonder how he was going to let Holly know that he was here. Kristian had to think of something fast. He couldn't just walk right up and knock on the door and ask for her, if her parents answered the door they would be questioning why a German would want to see Holly. "How am I going to let Holly know that I'm here?" Kristian said Decker, not having a clue what to do.

"Not a problem," Decker said. "There's a boy named Gabriel that lives right next door to her. He is always outside playing and he is how I get your letters to Holly."

"How is that?" Kristian said curiously. We have a deal that I'll pay him a little money every time he takes a letter to her, but he can't tell anyone," Decker said. "Oh, by the way. You owe me some money."

The boys reached Gabriel's house and as Decker predicted Gabriel was outside playing in the street in front of his house. "Gabriel," Decker yelled, waving at the boy to catch his attention. Gabriel stopped what he was doing and with a smile on his face ran to Decker. Gabriel was young enough not to have a fear or disdain for the Germans, to him they were just soldiers. And as with every other boy, had a love for the brave men with their weapons and sharp uniforms. To him, they were more of a novelty, something to admire and aspire to be. "Decker, Decker," the boy shouted as he ran, as if Decker was a playmate he hadn't seen in a while. The boy ran to Decker, and Decker squatted down and took a knee.

"Hey little buddy, how are you doing," Decker said the boy.

"I'm ok," the boy said. "Do you have another letter for Holly?"

"No, not today," Decker told the boy. "Today we are doing something a little different. You see my friend here?"

"Yes," the boy said.

"His name is Kristian," Decker told Gabriel.

"Hi Kristian," the boy said with a smile and a salute. Kristian smiled at the adorable little boy's greeting.

"Hello there Gabriel," Kristian said returning the boy's salute. Kristian is a friend of Holly's too, but he can't go to her house either. Will you go to Holly's house and tell her to come out and talk to us?"

"Yes, do I get some money and?" the boy asked.

"Of course, that's our deal, right?" Little Gabriel nodded his head yes.

"Remember, you can't tell anyone but Holly."

"Ok" Gabriel said then quickly darted to Holly's front door.

As the little boy ran to Holly's door, Kristian and Decker looked at each other and smiled at how cute that little boy was. Gabriel knocked on Holly's door and an old woman opened the door and greeted the boy with a smile and a pat on his young cheek. The old woman went back inside the house and a few seconds later Holly came to the door. Gabriel waved at Holly to bend down then whispered something in her ear and pointed where Kristian and Decker were standing. Holly saw Kristian and Decker, and an excited smile came over her face. Holly quickly stuck her head back in the house and shouted that she was going outside. Just as quickly she slammed the door closed behind her and ran smiling from ear to ear to where Kristian was standing.

Holly ran to Kristian eagerly and wanting to jump into his arms, but reluctantly restrained herself. They were too close to home and it was very likely they might be seen by a neighbor or even her family. "Follow me," Holly said, but not too close." Holly walked quickly down the road occasionally looking back to make sure Kristian was still following her. Holly walked around the back of a building and out of Kristian's sight. Kristian picked up his pace in an effort to catch up with Holly and as he went around the corner of the building Holly jumped on him, her arms around his neck and her legs wrapped around his waist. The weight of Holly and the unexpected force of her loving attack made Kristian fall to the ground. As Kristian lay on his back, Holly continued to sit straddling atop of Kristian kissing his face as if to devour him.

Seeing the passion that was being displayed before him, Decker turned his head and covered his eyes. "Uh, should I leave and come back later?" he asked, feeling like the proverbial third wheel.

Holly momentarily took a break from kissing Kristian and quickly looked up at Decker. "Yes, go away," Holly said, then just as quick, returned to devouring her prey. Decker shrugged his shoulders and surrendered to Holly's demand, turning around and slowly wandering away. "Holly…Holly," Kristian said struggling to break free from Holly's overpowering welcome. Holly raised up, pulling her face away from his. "What?" Holly said. "Not that I don't like your greeting, I do, but I'm lying on a rock and its killing me," Kristian groaned.

"Oh," Holly said with a look of both pain and sympathy on her face. "I'm so sorry." I think I broke a rib," Kristian said as he reached around to his back. "Let me take a look at it," Holly told Kristian. "No, I'll be ok; just give me a minute," Kristian said. "Don't be ridiculous, take off your tunic and lift your shirt, I want to have a look at it and make sure you

196

are ok," Holly said with a clearly instinctive, motherly command.

"Okay, okay," Kristian said complying with her demand. Kristian took off his tunic and pulled his shirt tails out of his trousers then lifted his shirt so that Holly could inspect his wound. Holly looked over Kristian's back.

"You're a big baby; there's barely a red spot on your back," Holly said in a scolding voice.

"Hey, it hurt," Kristian whined.

"I thought soldiers were trained to be tough," Holly said teasing Kristian.

"We are," Kristian said. "I just haven't had the rocks in our backs training yet."

Chapter Eighteen

Holly stood up and held out her hand, offering Kristian help up off the ground. "Come with me," Holly told Kristian with a sheepish smile. Kristian took hold of Holly's hand and allowed her to slightly help him off of the ground. "Where are we going?" Kristian asked, curious about what Holly had in mind to do. Again, Holly held her hand out for Kristian to take hold of, backspace. She began to guide him to her unspoken destination. "Where are we going?" Kristian said as he again took hold of Holly's hand.

"Never you mind, you just follow me. I promise you'll like it," Holly said with a smile and a tug of Kristian's arm. The two young lovers walked for ten minutes to the edge of town to a

198

wildflower covered meadow surrounded by a three-railed wood fence.

Kristian and Holly stood at the fence looking over it at the flower covered field. The warm spring breeze blew down upon the flowers making the flowers bow appearing like waves rolling across the beautiful multi colored meadow.

"Wow, this is very pretty. Is this what you wanted to show me?" Kristian said.

"No, come on," Holly told him as she began to climb over the fence into the field of flowers.

Kristian shrugged his shoulders, open to anything Holly would suggest to do. "Ok," Kristian said, and he too crawled over the wood fence. Once Kristian's feet touched the ground on the other side of the fence, Holly smiled at Kristian then quickly turned away and began to run through the field. Holly's arms were stretched out at her sides to touch the tops of the flowers as she ran, giggling and occasionally turning back to look at Kristian to entice him to chase after her.

More than willing to play the game, Kristian smiled and began to chase the beautiful and spirited girl that he had been so smitten by. Kristian and Holly ran into the field, weaving

through the flowers laughing until they reached the center of the

field. Kristian caught Holly, wrapping his arms around her waist,

gently pulling her to the ground. They lay side by side, laughing

immensely, enjoying the time that they were spending together.

Slowly their laughing subsided as they lay amid while the

flowers and began to look deeply into each other's eyes in

silence. Holly unexpectedly sprang upon Kristian and began

passionately kissing his lips. Holly tightly grasped a hand full of

Kristian's hair in both hands in effort to pull herself even closer

into Kristian in an attempt to ever more passionately deepen her

kiss.

Holly lay atop of Kristian, her legs spread straddling his

leg. Slowly Holly began grinding against Kristian's leg, lightly

moaning in pleasure as she continued to kiss him. Kristian

grabbed hold of Holly's firm ass and pulled her deeply into his

leg, aiding her with the rhythm of her grind. Holly moaned and

continued without interruption of her pleasure until she could no

longer resist her burning carnal desires. Holly sat up over

Kristian and began removing her blouse, struggling with each button that was normally effortless to undo. Kristian followed

suit sitting up ripping off his tunic and shirt, also struggling with

each button in his attempt to remove it as quickly as possible.

Just for a moment they stopped and viewed the creation of the

ecstasy they both were about to receive, then fell back into the

flowers that would conceal their intimacy from the rest of the

world.

  With the thirst of their desire quenched, the young lovers

began to dress. Kristian stopped for a moment and smiled at

Holly.

    "What?" Holly said with a smile and a tilt of her

head. Kristian reached over to Holly and pulled a

wildflower from her hair, then held it up in front of her,

rolling it back and forth between his fingers.

  "A flower, for you my sweet," Kristian said with a

smile.

    "You are a silly boy," Holly told Kristian as she

took the bluebell from his hand. "I need to get back

home before my mother comes looking for me," she said

with regret and disappointment on her face.

"Okay, I'll walk you back. Or at least close to your house," Kristian said.

"Okay," Holly replied. "Let's make sure the coast is clear before we get up." Kristian and Holly slowly raised their heads above the tops of the flowers, making sure no one was around to discover their secret rendezvous.

Confirming no one was around to discover them, Kristian and Holly looked at each other with devious smiles, elated that they got away with their forbidden deeds. "Come on, let's go," Holly told Kristian waving him to come with her. The young lovers walked hand in hand back to the village, swinging their grasped arms as they walked. "When do you think the Germans will leave France?" Holly said Kristian.

"Germany will never leave France; France is part of the Reich now," Kristian replied.

"France will never be part of the Reich," Holly said angrily.

"Look, the French are going to have to accept the fact that they have been conquered," Kristian said.

"France will never be conquered. I hate you," Holly said slapping Kristian's face. Kristian stood there shocked at Holly's reaction and watched her confused as she ran crying toward her home.

As Kristian stood there dumbfounded at Holly's reaction to his comments, questioning how she could love him and at the same time not want him here. An unexpected crack of lightning thundered from behind him causing Kristian to almost instinctively dive to the ditch beside the road due to being a bit punch-drunk from Allied air raids. Cool breezes blew past where Kristian was standing and he could smell that almost refreshing scent of rain in the air. "Crap," Kristian said to himself, knowing that soon he would be soaked to the bone from the rain. He quickly began to head to the delivery area where he and Decker had left the truck to be unloaded in order to get some sort of shelter from the storm.

When Kristian got to the supply dump the truck was no longer where he and Decker had left it. He walked around the nearby area searching but could not find Decker's truck. He went inside the receiving office to see if Decker might be held up inside trying to escape the oncoming storm. Kristian opened the door and walked inside to a small room, barely large enough for a desk and occupant with no spare room for chairs for visitors to sit in. Sitting behind the desk was a slightly overweight sergeant with a piece of chicken in one hand and a book in the other, leaning back comfortably in his chair with his feet propped atop of his desk, enjoying a quiet afternoon.

"Is Decker still around?" Kristian said the sergeant.

"Decker who?" the sergeant said with a snarl, upset that his serenity had been interrupted.

"Oh, I'm sorry. Decker Houst; he is a driver," Kristian replied.

"Oh, young Decker," the Sergeant said with a smile. "I'm sorry son, my head was still in my book. Decker left about an hour ago. If you want to catch him, he has a hell of a start on you," The Sergeant said with a light chuckle.

"Well, crap," Kristian said to himself as he looked down at the floor contemplating what he was going to do next and wondering how he was going to get back to camp. "Well, I guess I can just stay in here until the storm passes, or I can catch a ride with another driver," Kristian said both to himself and the sergeant.

"I'm afraid not sonny, there's not enough room in here for a bunch of strays to lounge around, we are just too busy here," the sergeant said to Kristian, clearly just because he didn't want Kristian to stay.

"But there's no one here," Kristian said shrugging his shoulders, looking around the little room. "I could have a mad rush of trucks any minute now, you're just going to have to move on boy," the sergeant said with a frown. Kristian gave the sergeant a very clear, "you're an asshole" look then opened the door, walked out and slammed the door behind him.

Kristian looked up into the darkening sky. "Looks like I'm going to get a little wet," Kristian said to himself then flipped up the collar of his tunic up around his neck, adjusted his cap, and began his journey back to camp.

As Kristian walked down the road it began to rain. Lightly at first, but then it quickly became a deluge of cool springtime water, soaking him to the bone. The rain soon gave Kristian a chill as he walked down the dirt road that was quickly turning to mud. Kristian's jackboots he had so carefully polished to a reflection giving shine the evening before began to be covered in mud, erasing every trace of the effort that he had put into his work. "Can this day get any worse?" Kristian groaned shaking his head at his misery. The lightning and thunder grew more heavily by the minute and with each flash of lighting he began to seriously fear for his safety.

In the distance Kristian began to hear the engine of a vehicle coming toward him from behind, luckily heading in his direction of travel. As the vehicle came closer Kristian could see that it was a *Kubelwagen* (Bucket Automobile) a name given for its bucket seats, but the troops lovingly just called it *Das Kubel* or (The Bucket). The car was a convertible, usually used as a staff car and was sturdy and reliable comparable to the American Jeep. As the car approached Kristian it slowed down and stopped beside him in the road. There was a young regular Army soldier

206

driving, wearing a helmet and desert goggles and soaked to the bone as well from the rain.

"You know you would stay dry if you put the roof up on the vehicle," Kristian told the driver sarcastically.

"Very funny, smart guy," the driver replied. "I can't get the damn thing up; it's jammed."

"Hop out, I'll give you a hand; maybe with the both of us working on it we can get it up," Kristian suggested. The driver nodded in agreement and jumped out of the car eagerly, willing to try in an effort to get out of the pouring rain. With the driver on one side of the vehicle and Kristian on the other they both grabbed the edge of the folding tarp roof and roughly pulled, jiggled and jerked until they finally got the roof free from whatever it was that was holding it down.

"Hey, hey," the driver said happily.

"Yeah, we got it," Kristian said rejoicing as well.

"What a team. Come on, let's get out of this damn rain," the driver told Kristian with a smile and a jerk of his head directing Kristian to get in the car. They both got in the vehicle and attempted to shake off the rain, but their efforts made little difference. Kristian and the driver looked up at the roof over their heads at the same time. "This is nice, so good to get out of that damn rain. To think I almost didn't stop, glad I did. Sometimes it pays to have a soft heart," the driver told Kristian.

"Well, I thank your soft heart," Kristian said. "My name is Kristian, what's yours?"

"My name is Amery," the driver replied.

Kristian stuck out his hand to shake Amery's. "Damn glad to meet you and grateful you came along."

Amery took Kristian's hand and with a smile gave it a hearty shake. "I guess we both had the opportunity to make someone else's life a little better today," Amery told Kristian. "It's the Christian thing to do," he said smiling at Kristian, letting him know that the pun was clearly intended.

"Ah, I got it, cute," Kristian said. Amery smiled at Kristian's response as he ground the gearshift in the

208

transmission putting the Kubel into first gear. "I take it you're one of those religious fellows," Kristian said to Amery.

"You could say that I guess," Amery said. "I've never really needed God or any of that superstitious kind of stuff," Kristian told Amery.

"Oh, you do," Amery said. "You just don't know it yet."

Chapter Nineteen

Back at camp the following morning Kristian awoke to the lights of the billets being turned on and a sergeant yelling in the door. "Get your asses out of bed, get your gear and weapons and fall out in front of the building. Move it ladies we don't have all day, move it, move it." All the boys jumped out of their bunks and quickly began getting dressed and grabbing their equipment. "What the hell time is it?" Kristian said Gunny as they both scurried around half asleep clumsily trying to get dressed.

Gunny looked at his watch. "three a.m.," Gunny said in disbelief. "I wonder what the hell is going on?" Kristian said.

"Hell, I don't know," Gunny said. "I guess we will find out soon enough though. If they're waking us up this early, whatever it is, it sure as hell isn't good."

One by one the boys ran out of the billets and lined up in formation in front of the building, many of the boys still tucking in their shirts, buttoning their pants or fumbling around with their gear. "Listen up," the sergeant bellowed to the platoon. "We have received information that the partisans are planning an attack on the railway. We are told that they're held up in the Village of Lisiex. Our job is to go door to door and find these little bastards and execute them as an example of what will be done to anyone that attempts to resist the Reich. There will be no exceptions, and no mercy shown. It must be very clear to the people of France that this will not be tolerated, and if they're foolish enough to do so, they will quickly reap what they sow."

Four Opel Blitz three-ton troop trucks drove up accompanied by two 234 Puma heavy armored cars each armed with a 1x2 KwK 39 cannon and a MG 34 machine-gun, plenty of firepower to overcome any ambitious lightly armed partisans. The small convoy pulled up and stopped in front of the platoon's

211

formation. "Get your asses loaded up in the trucks," the sergeant yelled at the platoon. The boys broke up into squads, each squad loading in its own single truck. The sergeant walked down the line of vehicles making sure that all of the men were loaded in the trucks, properly positioned and alert for any possible ambush along the route. The sergeant then climbed into the Kfz 15 Horch command vehicle with the platoon leader, then stood in the front seat and waved for the column to move out following his vehicle.

The troop truck that Kristian was riding in pulled away with a neck snapping jerk and a grinding of the gears. "Son of a bitch, who the hell is driving this thing?" One of the boys groaned as he rubbed his neck from the painful jolt.

"Probably a new replacement," another boy said. "I don't think they even bother training these guys how to drive anymore, they just throw them in a truck and point them in the direction they want them to go." As the small convoy wound down the narrow roads to Lisiex, the sun began to rise, exposing a blue sky lightly spotted with fluffy clouds colored a light red and orange from the rays of the morning sun. The breeze blowing through the truck was cool and the air smelled fresh from the previous night's rain. "It's going to be a beautiful day," Kristian said loudly to the boy sitting next to him, trying to be heard over the sound of the truck's engines. "Yeah, maybe that's a sign we are going to have a good day," the boy said optimistically.

The troop trucks and armored vehicles drove into the center of the village of Lisiex and came to a halt in the middle of the street. Immediately, the boys began to jump out of the truck and line up in formation for instructions. Once the platoon was formed, the sergeant stood before them and began to give them the orders of the day. "Men, I want you to form up into teams of two and go door to door searching each house, checking the inhabitant's papers and looking for anyone suspicious. We know that some of the villagers are giving aid to the partisans. Those villagers, as well as the partisans, are to be shot. When you find them, bring them to the center of the village. They will be held there until the town is clear and then we will deal with them from there. Understood?"

"Yes sergeant," the platoon said in unison.

213

The platoon broke up into teams of two and Kristian was
unlucky enough to get paired up with Einhard Earnst. Einhard
was one of those guys who didn't give a crap about anyone but
himself. He was a heartless, cruel bully with no compassion for
any living thing, man nor beast. Scuttlebutt around the platoon
was that the only reason he had joined the SS was so that he
could freely kill people without being sent to prison. A real
sweetheart. Kristian was not enthused with who he had been
paired with, and it was clearly written all over his face. "What's
the matter with you, you look like you just swallowed a bug,"
Einhard replied.

"Don't worry about it," Kristian said. "Let's just go and
do what we have to do,"

Kristian didn't like Einhard at all, so he always called
him by his last name, Earnst. It was an effort to let him know
that he was not considered a friend, just someone that he was
forced to work with. Kristian had had run ins with Earnst before,
defending the smaller boys in the platoon from his bullying and
there was no love lost between them. "Come on, let's go knock

214

off a few of these little French bastards," Earnst said with a smile and a gleam in his eyes.

"Slow down there, dumbass, don't get in too big of a hurry. If you're not careful you can get yourself killed, even worse, get me killed," Kristian told Earnst.

"Don't be a sissy," Earnst said. "There isn't a Frenchman alive that's man enough to kill me."

Kristian and Earnst went to the door of the first house, took the butt of his rifle and began banging it on the door. "Open the door," Earnst commanded to whoever was inside the home. Earnst again began banging on the door with the butt of his riffle. "Open up or we will break the door down," Earnst ordered the occupants of the home. A little old woman slowly opened the door peeking to see who was at the door and as it opened, Earnst kicked the door open knocking the old woman to the floor.

"Who else is here?" Earnst said the woman with a violent tone in his voice.

"There's no one here but me," the old woman said. Kristian walked just inside the door and watched as Earnst began searching the small home, unnecessarily

215

throwing things across the room and breaking the few items the old woman owned.

"No, no," the old women said waving her hand. "There's no one here but me."

"Hey, asshole, let's go," Kristian told Earnst. "Clearly there's no one here."

"That old bitch could be one of them," Earst said, still rummaging through the old woman's things. Kristian walked over to Earnst and roughly grabbed his arm and pulled him in the direction of the door.

"Hey, what the hell?" Earnst said.

"Get outside, dumbass, she's alone and you're just being an asshole," Kristian told Earnst as he manhandled him out of the front door. Kristian stopped just inside the doorway and looked at the little old woman on the floor crying into her hands. The old woman looked up at Kristian, his face clearly showing shame at what had just taken place.

Kristian could no longer look into her face and lowered his eyes to the floor as he shook his head with sympathy.

Kristian began to walk out of the little house and noticed a small photograph in a hand carved wood frame lying in the doorway. The photo was of an infant in a small coffin. Kristian bent down, picked up the photo, and looked deeply into the child's face. Kristian looked over at the old woman who was watching him as he looked at the photograph. Kristian could tell that the child was someone very dear to the old woman by the expression on her face. He looked into the woman's sad and remorseful eyes and gently handed the photo to her, then slowly walked out of the house, quietly closing the door behind him.

Kristian and Earnst walked to the next house and Earnst repeated his violent process of banging the butt of his rifle on the door demanding the inhabitants to open the door. Suddenly the door of the house opened and two men came bolting out from inside the house, one of the men running to the left and the other to the right. Earnst chased after the man that began running to the left and Kristian took after the man that went to the right. The man Kristian was chasing was too fast for him to catch, so he stopped running and took aim at the back of the man. "Halt,"

Kristian yelled to the man. "Halt or I'll shoot." But the man continued to run.

Kristian fired a warning shot just over the man's head yet he continued to run, ignoring the warning. Kristian raised his rifle and took aim at dead center of the man's back and fired a shot. The round from the rifle hit its mark, entering the man's back and exiting through his chest, killing him instantly. His lifeless body fell to the ground and a thick pool of blood began surrounding his upper torso.

"Excellent shot Ackmann," Kristian's sergeant shouted from the other side of the road.

"Good job young man, keep it up, we'll make a killer out of you yet." The sergeant's praise fell on deaf ears. Kristian wasn't proud of what he had done and it didn't feel good taking another man's life. Kristian's feelings confused him and he began to doubt his ability to be a good soldier. For some reason he didn't have that bloodlust that he was trained to have.

"Ackmann, move out and check the next house," the sergeant yelled. Kristian went to the next house alone and just as he got to the door it opened and a man ran out knocking Kristian to the ground as he ran by. The man ran around the corner of the house and out of sight. Kristian quickly got to his feet and began to give chase, running around the corner of the building after the possible escaping partisan. He ran down the side of the house then turned the corner going into the back yard but did not see the man that was running from him. The yard was fenced in with two large storage sheds in the yard and bushes all around that could easily conceal a hiding man.

Kristian raised his rifle ready to fire and began searching around the yard. Kristian carefully and quietly walked around the bushes, listening for any sound that might give his prey away. Kristian slowly walked around the first shed peeking around each corner of the shack before proceeding to walk around it. The sound of stacked boards being knocked over and falling to the ground came from behind the second shed, giving away the position of the man Kristian was searching for. Kristian slowly walked over to the shed, rifle ready to fire at anyone that might threaten him. Kristian walked to the back side of the shed where the noise had come from, and he spotted a man attempting to climb over the fence.

"Halt," Kristian loudly ordered. The man climbed down from the fence still facing away from Kristian. "Turn around slowly," Kristian ordered. The man slowly turned to where Kristian could see his face. Shock came over Kristian and he could not believe what he was seeing. It was Henry, Holly's cousin. Kristian lowered his rifle, not sure what to do, then came to the realization that Henry was a partisan and again raised his rifle and took aim. "Aim true Kristian," Henry said as a dying request, then fell to his knees and began to pray.

Kristian carefully aimed his rifle at the center of Henry's forehead ensuring instant death. Kristian stood aiming at Henry for several seconds, confused on what to do. Henry was clearly the enemy, but he was also Holly's cousin. He was Holly's family and at some point, he could be family of his as well. Kristian lowered his rifle and seeing this, Henry stopped praying. "Go," Kristian told him, pointing his rifle in the direction that he should run. Henry got to his feet. "I guess prayer works," Henry said with a smile.

"Either that or your just damn lucky," Kristian said smiling back at Henry.

"I guess all of you bastards aren't bad," Henry said with a grateful look on his face.

"Get out of here," Kristian told Henry, then turned and walked away.

Chapter Twenty

From the end of May through the first few days of June, there had been an increase in radio transmissions on Allied radio stations to the French resistance organizations. German counter intelligence had learned that the French resistance movement would be informed through the British radio station, The BBC, of the date that the invasion of France by the Allies would come. Special coded messages for each resistance group were created and were to be sent in two parts as to confuse German intelligence. Transmitting the first part meant that the invasion would occur within two weeks, and when the second part of the message was transmitted the invasion would begin within 48 hours.

On June 1st the Allies transmitted 125 messages containing the first part of the message, and German intelligence monitoring those transmissions recognized that the invasion would be within 14 days. It was also revealing that the messages were sent to resistance groups in the Brittany, Normandy area ruling out an invasion at the presumed point at the Pas de Calais. Knowing this information, German command ordered all fighting positions be reinforced with sandbags, camouflaged and manned prepared for the oncoming invasion. Kristian was detailed out to build a pillbox using timber and sandbags next to the road barricade, so that machine-guns could sweep the enemy if they were unfortunate enough to venture toward their position.

Kristian and the other boys on the work detail were shirtless due to the heat, their bodies covered in sweat and dirt from their exhausting labor. Kristian was shoveling sand from a pile that a truck had dropped off next to where the pillbox was to be built. He and the other boys filling the sand bags one by one, each with several shovel loads of sand. Focused on the job at hand and the misery of working in the heat under direct sunlight,

Kristian did not hear the car pulling up to the checkpoint from behind him. "Kristian."

Kristian thought that he heard someone call his name, but he wasn't sure if he actually heard it or if was just his imagination playing tricks on him as he worked.

"Kristian," someone called again.

This time Kristian clearly heard a woman's voice calling his name and turned to see who it was.

He saw Holly standing next to her father's car, waving at him with a smile acting as if she was ecstatic to see him. Kristian, a bit confused, smiled back at Holly as he thought to himself. "Well, I guess she must be over being mad at me." Still happy to see her nonetheless, he tossed his shovel onto the pile of sand and at a quick pace walked over to Holly and began to give her a hug. Holly raised her arms and with her hands on his chest, pushed Kristian back in order to stop him from hugging her. "You're filthy," Holly said with a stink face. "No hugs, just a kiss." Kristian's face gave away his disappointment and Holly sympathetically reneged her demand. "Come here," Holly told

Kristian holding her arms open wide to receive Kristian's wanted affection.

Holding their loving embrace, Kristian then pulled away and gave Holly a quick kiss, a little embarrassed expressing such affection in front of all of his comrade's peering eyes. Holly looked down at her dress and began brushing off the dirt Kristian's hug gave her.

"What are you doing here?" Kristian said.

"I had to come see you," Holly said. "I had to tell you that I was sorry, I overreacted. Will you forgive me?"

"Don't be silly," Kristian said with a loving smile. "Of course, I will, you don't even have to ask."

"I also wanted to tell you thank you."

"For what?" Kristian said.

"For saving Henry," she replied.

"You're welcome, and he's welcome; just don't ever mention it again," Kristian told her with raised brow.

"He would have come and thanked you himself, but he thought it might not be safe for him or you," Holly explained.

"Tell him, don't worry about it. Tell him that he owes me a good bottle of wine," Kristian said with a smile.

Holly put her arms around Kristian again and gave him a hug with a tight squeeze. "I love you, Kristian," Holly lovingly told him.

"Listen," Kristian said, grabbing Holly's arms half way between shoulder and elbow to get her undivided attention. Rumor has it that the Allies will be coming any day now. I may not get to see you for a while."

"Why, what, I don't understand. Will you be leaving?" Holly said.

"No, we will be staying for now; That's what I'm doing now, we are kind of reinforcing our positions just in case," he tried to explain. "I'm sorry, but I can't tell you any more than that."

"Kristian, I'm scared for you," Holly said sincerely. "If they come, run away. Leave, go somewhere safe."

"I can't do that Holly, I'm a soldier," he told her. "Soldiers don't run, they fight, and we will win. You'll see, so don't worry, I'll be fine."

Holly again hugged Kristian tightly, burying her head deep into Kristian's chest.

Kristian reluctantly pulled Holly away from him. "Now, you are going to have to go, sweetheart," Kristian told her.

"I don't want to. Can't we spend a little time together?" Holly asked almost begging.

"I'm afraid we can't, Holly. I've to get back to work and you being here right now is a little suspicious," Kristian told Holly. "But I'll come see you as soon as I possibly can. I promise."

"Okay," Holly said with a pout.

Kristian opened the car door and Holly got inside and started the engine. Kristian leaned down and

227

kissed Holly's lips one last time, not knowing, if he would be alive to ever kiss them again knowing the invasion was soon to come. "I'll come see you as soon as I can, I promise," Kristian told her in reassurance.

"You better mister," Holly replied with a smile, poorly attempting to hide her pain. Kristian stepped away from the car and watched Holly turn the vehicle around on the road then stood in the middle of the road watching Holly drive away.

"Hey, lover boy," One of the boys in his work detail hollered. "Get your ass back over here and get to work." Kristian smiled at the boy, shaking his head, then slowly returned to his backbreaking work.

That evening around ten p.m., German intelligence intercepted a British message to the French Resistance. The message consisted of one stanza of a poem by Verlaine which read, roughly translated: "*The long sobbing of the violins in autumn, it wounds my heart with its monotonous melancholy.*" This message gave the Germans confirmation that the invasion would begin within 48 hours, giving them ample time to prepare.

Brigadefuhrer (Brigadier General) Witt, Commander of the HJ Division and his staff were relaxing, sitting by the fireplace at the house of the commander enjoying cognac and cigars. Around midnight it was reported to command that the Allies had dropped straw dolls by parachute in army uniforms in a deceiving maneuver near the airfields.

There were no other reports of airborne landings, so the German commander determined that the Allies were testing the Germans for information concerning their reactions to an airborne assault, and initially dismissed the report. An hour and a half later it was reported that paratroopers of unknown strength, had landed near the area of Troarn. At three a.m. Kristian's division receive code word "Blucher" alerting them that the Anglo-Americans had landed, and the men were quickly assembled. The platoon sergeant burst into the billets shouting at the boys to get up. "Let's go boys, get up," the sergeant yelled. "The Tommies have landed."

"Is this another night exercise?" One of the boys said complaining, not asking anyone in particular. "Is this for real?" "Do you think this is the real thing?"

Kristian said Gunny, his heart pounding with excitement.

"No, they wouldn't dare," Gunny replied, rolling his eyes. "Don't get your hopes up my friend, it's probably another drill just like all the others we've done week after week after week."

"Hey, sergeant," Kristian yelled getting the sergeant's attention. "Is this another drill, or the real thing?"

"This is the real shit boy, so you better get your ass together, get your kit and fall in out front for your orders." Kristian and Gunny looked at each other wide eyed, surprised and in disbelief.

"Shit," Gunny said excitedly then jumped up from his bunk and frantically started dressing and gathering his gear.

Kristian followed suit. "Are you ready for this?" Kristian asked Gunny.

"I hope the hell so," Gunny said.

"We sure as hell have trained enough for it, but I'm not really happy about the idea of one of those Tommies taking a shot at me."

"Just keep your head down and your ass next to me," Kristian told Gunny. "And don't do anything stupid, I need somebody covering my ass," he said with a reassuring smile. "I'm not sure if I trust any other of these idiots to do the job."

"Don't you worry, I'll keep you alive," Gunny said. "You still have to get Holly to introduce me to one of her friends."

"You got it," Kristian said with a smile and a pat on Gunny's shoulder. "As soon as we wrap this up, we will be double dating before you know it."

The platoon was formed outside in front of the billets, and the platoon leader began to inform the boys of the situation at hand. "Men, we have word that airborne troops have landed at several locations in the Normandy area. Their mission is to capture area bridges and river crossings in an attempt to stop reinforcements from reaching the coast. Allied forces are expected to attempt a beach landing at daylight and if needed, we will be sent to reinforce our troops in an effort to keep the Allies from getting a foothold on the coast. I don't expect that we will be needed but be ready to move out at a moment's notice. That is all," the lieutenant ordered, then he sharply turned around and headed back to division headquarters.

The boy's broke formation and went back to their quarters until they received further instructions. All of the boys stretched out on their bunks but continued to stay prepared to move out at a moment's notice. Those who could, slept. The others were talking quietly or playing cards. At daybreak the sergeant reentered the billets and said, "All right boys, I want you to go outside and load up into the APC's (armored personnel carriers) in preparation to move out. We may be getting orders to support troops defending bridges near Caen. If for some reason we are overwhelmed and have to retreat, our orders will be to blow the bridges before we leave the area. We cannot afford to allow those bridges to fall into the hands of the Allies. Move out."

"Well, I guess this is it," Kristian told Gunny. "It's finally happening."

"Yeah, we have been expecting this for quite a while though," Gunny said. "This is what we have been preparing for for months."

"I know," Kristian said with a slight sense of dread on his face. "I truly hoped it would never come though. I hoped we could sit out the war right here until we worked out a peace treaty or something with the allies."

"Well, it looks like that is not going to happen," Gunny said shaking his head. "Don't worry Kristian, there's no way the Allies can get enough men on the beach to take it. It's going to be like shooting fish in a barrel, and the airborne troops don't stand a chance. They're surrounded on all sides and there isn't anywhere for them to go, but to the grave."

Chapter Twenty-one

At 1:30 a.m. the Allies had sent approximately 100 bombers to obliterate eight German gun batteries along the coast, dropping 500-600 tons of bombs on each target. Surprisingly, there was minimal damage to the bunkered guns, and at 5 a.m. the Allied battle ships and cruisers began to open fire on the German front lines. The undamaged coastal guns returned fire and the exchange lasted for hours, but the ship's superior artillery prevailed. The American troops began hitting the beach around 6:30 a.m. followed at 7:30 a.m. by the Canadians near Bernieres, engaging in heavy combat with German infantry positions. The 12th SS HJ Division wasn't released to aid in the defense until 2:30 p.m., giving the Allies ample time to get a strong foothold on the Normandy coastline.

The HJ were still not fully equipped; they had no tank destroyers and the mortar units had no tractors to pull the guns. The platoon sergeant walked up and called the boys out of the APC's into formation for a briefing. "Here we go," Gunny said to Kristian. "I bet we are going to head out now."

"I hope so," Kristian said. "This waiting around crap is for the birds, hell, I would rather be facing the Tommies than wasting time here." The boys climbed out of the vehicle and quickly got into formation, eager to get the word they were moving out. Many of them eager and chomping at the bit to get the opportunity to put the training that they have been doing for months into action and finally get to fight.

Once the platoon stood silently in formation, the sergeant began to give them the orders of the day. "Men, as Panzer scouts we must be quick and agile. We must see everything and not be seen. Our machine-guns are only to be used in defense. If you open fire you give your position away and remember, you are not sitting in the protection of a tank.

That tunic you are wearing gives you absolutely no protection from enemy fire, so keep your asses down. Pay attention to the road surfaces, Partisans are well known for ambushing with mines and today, undoubtedly, they will be in increased numbers. March sequence will be, one squad of motorcycle riflemen will lead, followed by 8 wheelers and 4 wheelers keeping a distance of 50 meters between them at all times, then one squad of motorcycle riflemen bringing up the rear. All right men, load up."

Kristian and Gunny climbed back into the APC and got as comfortable as they could for the journey to the front. "Woo hoo, we are finally on our way, Gunny said to Kristian. "Aren't you excited?"

"Actually, I'm a little excited and a little scared shitless," Kristian replied.

"It is starting to get serious now," Gunny smiled and patted Kristian on the back in reassurance. "Don't worry my friend I got your back, so you have absolutely nothing to worry about." Kristian gave Gunny a not so assured smile then looked down at the floorboard of the vehicle and became deep in thought of what was to come. Did he have the guts and was he strong enough to be a good soldier? Only time would tell.

The order came to move out and the column of vehicles began heading to their assigned area of security. The vehicles traveled at a leisurely 40 kilometers per hour and the morning was cool, pleasant, and the moon could still be seen occasionally popping through breaks in the fog and clouds. Visibility fluctuated between 50 and 100 meters and after only a couple of kilometers it began to feel just like the many practice alarms they had had over the weeks. The few houses they passed as they went through the villages were quiet, the inhabitants still inside sleeping. There was no signs of the expected partisans and the boys were all feeling quite at ease.

The vehicles stopped at the Abteilung command post to receive orders for their mission. "Alright men, out of the vehicles and in formation," the sergeant bellowed. All the boys quickly jumped out of the 4 and 8 wheelers and lined up in formation. "Men, we will be split up into four scouting parties," the sergeant said. "The first scout party will march via Bernay,

Lieureyand into Point L' Evique area, also including the coastal areas of Villers-sur-Mer and Deauville to Honfleur. The second group will take Lisieux, Branville and the coastal area of Houlgate, Dives, Cabourg and east of the mouth of the Orn River. Third Group will take the Caen area, and west of the Orn river up to St. Aubin. The fourth will take Bayeux area and the eastern coast to Courseulles,"

Emphasizing the importance of not being discovered by the Allies, the sergeant told the platoon, "I want you to report your positions hourly, and if you come into contact with the enemy as well. Avoid fighting if you can and bring back any prisoners immediately. I cannot stress this enough; secrecy is of utmost importance. That's all men, fall out."

"I guess we are going to have to be on our toes from here on," Kristian quietly said to Gunny.

"True, but we still have quite a ride until we get there," Gunny said. "At least I hope we are riding in the trucks there. I would hate to have to hump it there, that's another 60 kilometers away."

"We would probably wear out our boots before we got there," Kristian said, jokingly nudging Gunny with his elbow.

"Load up in the 8 wheelers men, we are moving out," the sergeant yelled.

The boys climbed in the trucks and began to make their way to Caen. The fog came and went on the route, at some points the eyes of the boys would water and their faces would bead like sweat from the thick cool fog. Columns of regular Army soldiers were passing by, heading in the opposite direction away from the advancing Allied forces. "Where the hell are they going?" Gunny said with a disgusted frown on his face. "Are they running from the enemy?"

"No, they can't be," Kristian said. "They would be shot for cowards. They must be regrouping for an attack or an ambush. It has to be something like that."

"What the hell are we heading that way for, are we just going to be cannon fodder so they will have the opportunity to regroup?" Gunny said, clearly not happy about the situation they were about to get themselves into.

"No, like the sergeant said," Kristian said. "We are going to be scouts, only confirming where the enemy is, their strength and direction of attack, nothing more. Hopefully, if we do our job right, we won't have any problems at all." Kristian was trying to ease Gunny's mind.

Gunny looked at Kristian with a frown, not reassured from Kristian's explanation at all. "I've a feeling it is going to be just a little more than a scouting expedition," Gunny said. "I've a feeling all hell is about to break loose."

When the column reached Caen, they drove through the center of the town. It was pure chaos, vehicles of all types were going in different directions with no sense of order. All of the boys in the transports were watching in disbelief from every point of the compass at the madness that was taking place before them. "What the hell is going on now?" Kristian said confused. "Isn't anyone in charge of these idiots? This is insane." The explosions from artillery guns and the sound of small arms weapons could be heard in the distance, confirming that the enemy was advancing quickly toward Caen. Kristian and Gunny looked at each other as did the rest of the boys with expressions of fear, disbelief and dread.

Kristian began inspecting his rifle, pulling the receiver back making sure it was functioning properly; he had to make sure that it would work without malfunctioning. He knew if a rifle doesn't fire, you might as well just carry a stick. The rest of the boys seeing Kristian, began checking their weapons as well. They knew that soon they would undoubtedly be in a kill or be killed situation, and there would be no room for mistakes. The whining engines of two diving British De Havilland Mosquito fighter-bombers caught the attention of every soldier on the street, instantly putting the fear of God in each one of them. Both aircraft opened up with their Browning machine-guns, strafing everything down the chaotic street, ripping men apart and exploding vehicles that were unfortunate enough to be in the line of fire.

Heavy black smoke from the burning vehicles began filling the street, choking the men and reducing visibility. Civilians began running out of the buildings in an effort to escape the devastation and death that was soon to come. Coughing and gasping for air, Kristian and the other boys tried to lay in the floorboard of the transport truck in an effort to get low enough to escape the noxious fumes of the burning vehicles. The scout trucks began to make a hasty exit out of the city, running over the bodies of dead and wounded soldiers. Their 8-wheeler occasionally had to plow through wrecked and burning vehicles in a desperate attempt to get out of the line of fire of the Mosquitos, and away from the deadly, bellowing, thick black smoke.

As the vehicles left town, the clear skies the boys had been wanting earlier letting the sun shine brightly on them. Fog was still drifting in from the coast, but it was to the right of the road. The boys were now praying the fog would again drift over them in order to conceal them from the deadly attacks of the Allied aircraft. "Where are our fighters?" Gunny said looking around in the sky. "We need protection from the Allied planes,"

242

"They're probably busy dogfighting them out on the coast," Kristian said. "I'm sure it is a hell of a lot worse there than it is here." The column continued unmolested to St. Sulpice and as they pulled into the village, the boys stood up in the vehicles to see if they could catch a glimpse of the action that was ensuing not far from town.

To the left, in the direction of the coast near Tracy, they could see burning houses, and columns of dirt rising from the explosions of artillery shells fired from Allied ships. The line of vehicles stopped and the sergeant stepped out of the first truck. "Everyone, out of the trucks and form into one column," Kristian and Gunny looked at each other, both with an "Oh boy, here we go," expression on their faces, then quickly complied to the sergeant's orders. The boys were marched about 1,000 meters to the highest point in the terrain, close to Magny-en-Bessin where they found a barn surrounded by trees to conceal them and a clear view across the bay of Arromanches.

"Oh my God Gunny, look at that," Kristian said looking out at the bay. The scout patrol beheld an unbelievable spectacle of a large grey mass of ships spreading out to the horizon.

243

Flashes were seen coming in various spots from naval artillery. Nearby houses and buildings were exploding, dirt and debris flying five stories in the air. Landing craft from the ships carrying hundreds of Allied soldiers were speeding toward the beachhead. Without any doubt the invasion was unstoppable, and it wouldn't be long until they were completely overrun. An uncontrollable inner feeling of terror came over all of the men; it was clear to see that this was the beginning of the end.

Chapter Twenty-two

As the landing craft hit the beaches, platoons of men came rushing out, screaming their battle cry and firing their weapons. Their helmets were flat, marking them as Brits. "The Tommies are landing boys," the sergeant yelled to the platoon. "Stay down and concealed, remember we are only to engage if absolutely necessary." The sergeant then called for the radioman. The radioman ran to the sergeant from the middle of the line of the platoon. "Call headquarters. Let them know our location, enemy strength and assessed damage to coastal batteries. Tell them without a doubt, the invasion is on."

The German MG-42 machine-gun began to open fire on the attacking British soldiers, its operator determined not to give

245

an inch of ground that wasn't paid for in blood. Platoons, then companies of enemy soldiers began slowly making their way over the dunes and off the beaches. The Brits were still 3,000 meters away and occasionally the smoke from the burning houses covered the view of the beach. After several minutes of the view being obstructed there was a break and the beach became clear to see. Tanks were now rolling onto the beaches in packs, firing on small pockets of German resistance. Artillery rounds began raining down all around Kristian's position, and mountains of dirt were being thrown into the air. It was clear that they must have been discovered, but by whom?

Whomever had discovered their position, must have called for an artillery barrage. But to be seen they would have to be close by and they would also have had to call the artillery strike upon their own position, a suicidal action. Kristian began to look around in an effort to spot whomever it was that gave them away but saw no one but the silhouette of a woman in the second story window of an old farm house. Seeing her standing there was surreal, it was if she were staring out to sea patiently waiting and pining for her lover to come and claim her. The explosion of another artillery round jolted Kristian back to reality, and the platoon began to run to the vehicles for safety from flying shrapnel.

The artillery barrage suddenly stopped in order to not endanger the advancing Allies. There was no doubt by the clear sound of small arms fire, that the Brits had made it to the road along the coastline behind the defensive batteries. Overhead the hum of Allied aircraft could be heard above the clouds and minutes later huge plumes of smoke could be seen rising high above Caen. "Oh my God," Kristian said to Gunny. "Look, they're bombing the shit out of Caen."

"Yeah," Gunny said. "There's going to be a hell of a lot of dead civilian men, women and children. They didn't get much warning and I'm sure they never thought they would get blown to bits by someone who is telling them that they're trying to save them."

The unit was ordered to immediately proceed to the bridge crossing the Dives River just behind Troarn. Fighter-bombers harassed the column along the way, but luckily, they had made it to their objective unharmed. In the pastures to the right and left of the road lay an unexpected surprise for the scouting team. Enemy transport gliders, though torn apart from Rommel's Asparagus, still had many combat ready survivors laying in ambush for the patrol. Using the wooden gliders for cover, the British commandos began shooting at the column with small arms fire. The patrol returned fire with 2 cm guns, firing explosive shells and incendiary grenades catching the wood gliders ablaze and killing several of the paratroopers.

The patrol continued returning fire at the British as they attempted to quickly cross the bridge over the Dives River and discovered that it had been completely destroyed. The vehicles in the column turned around on the road, still exchanging fire with the British soldiers and sped away in search of another route over the river. A railroad bridge was discovered not far away that crossed the river; it would be dangerous, but there were no other options. One by one the vehicles began to cross the train bridge. There were no rails or spikes and the vehicles bounced violently as they rolled over and between the wood planks laid across the bridge. Moving slow and high above the terrain, they were easy targets for ground troops as well as aircraft.

The column was receiving fire from the British below
the bridge, and immediately began to return fire. Accuracy was
virtually impossible bouncing along the tracks, and hitting the
enemy would only be achieved purely out of luck. Dive bombers
could be seen patrolling overhead and the situation look bleak
for the patrol, but by the grace of God they were not spotted by
the Allied aircraft. Kristian's vehicle reached the other side of
the bridge and the men in the vehicle all heavily sighed with
relief. "I'll never forget that," Kristian told Gunny. "I didn't
know if we were going to write ourselves off to heaven or hell,
but I'm damn glad it wasn't either."

"You and me both, brother," Gunny said. "When
I saw those aircraft, I thought we were dead men."

During training it was like children playing cowboys and
Indians, but now it had become deadly serious. One of the
fighter bombers spotted the column and began a dive to strafe
the vehicles to kill as many men as possible. The men were
trained to be the hunters, but now they were feeling what it was
like to be the rabbit. The machine-gunner in the 8-wheeler raised
his weapon and took aim at the attacking aircraft and fired off a

burst of rounds. The first set missed the target, but the machine-gunner's next burst hit the target spot on, killing the pilot. The aircraft continued its dive, crashing beside the column in a huge explosion throwing shrapnel and aircraft parts in every direction.

The second fighter bomber either had no ammunition or was so in shock at the fate of his comrade that he pulled the nose of his aircraft up and disappeared into the horizon. The boys in the vehicles broke out in cheers howling, whistling and slapping each other on the back for their unknowingly short-lived victory. It slowly became nightfall and the trek began to turn into a ghostly drive. Occasionally signal flares would be fired into the sky eliminating the convoy to be attacked from the woods by the Allied infantry and paratroopers hidden within. Finally, the scouting party escaped the enemy occupied area and turned south, headlights still nearly completely shielded, in the direction of Troarn-Caen.

After a short rest, the men were fed hard biscuits, tinned fish and coffee and allowed a little sack time. Their new marching orders from Command came in. The orders were to form a defensive/offensive line on both sides of Evrecy, 8.5

kilometers southwest of Caen, and if possible, recapture Flers-Vire and push the enemy back into the sea. "Well, we will finally get the opportunity to fight the enemy head on," Gunny said to Kristian. "I'm already tired of fleeing for my life, that's not what a soldier is trained to do."

"Be careful what you wish for my friend, you just might get it," Kristian said. "It's not going to be a cakewalk, we are outnumbered and they're better equipped. We just may have to get used to being on the run."

Along the route to their post, they were again harassed by fighter bombers and exchanged fire with the aircraft with little losses to their patrol. Occasionally they would come upon another unit, usually regular Army, that had been attacked by the Allied meat flies and ripped to shreds. This would slow the columns progress by having to stop and move destroyed vehicles, equipment and dead from the road. Kristian and Gunny were carrying bodies to the side of the road out of the path of the vehicles, and the sights and smells of the dead men made them feel ill. "God, Kristian, I don't know how much of this I'm going to be able to take, I feel like I'm going to puke."

"Hang in their buddy," Kristian said. "We should be done soon, and then we will be on our way."

"Where the hell is the air force; I've seen absolutely no air support," Gunny complained.

"Probably on the Eastern Front fighting the Russians," Kristian said.

"Well what about us?' Gunny said. "We are being slaughtered like pigs at a butcher."

"I don't know," Kristian said. "Perhaps they're regrouping for some kind of major counter attack."

"They're not going to have any troops to counter attack with, if they don't get us some kind of support soon," Gunny complained.

"Let's just take care of the job at hand," Kristian said. "Then we will tackle the crap we come across, one at a time."

"I guess we don't have much of a choice, do we?" Gunny said. Then the boys continued moving the dead soldiers from the road.

The boys once again heard the all too familiar hum of many aircraft engines coming their way and most of the scout patrol dove into the ditches beside the road, others ran into the woods for cover. Kristian and the other men looked up to the sky to see the oncoming assault and recognized the black Balken Cross on the fuselage and wings of the aircraft. "Those our ours," one of the boys shouted excitedly. They were ME 109's, 30 to 40 of them roaring by at low altitude. All of the men came out from cover and began waving at the pilots, while jumping and shouting, "Hurrah" and any other shouts of enthusiasm the boys could think of. "I wonder if they see us?" one of the boys said out loud.

One of the ME 109's passing by raised the nose of the aircraft and performed a loop above them. Then as the aircraft roared over their heads making its second pass, the pilot waved his wings as the aircraft flew by. "They were so low I could see the face of the pilots," Gunny said smiling ear to ear, utterly ecstatic to see them. "Now we have some support. Now things are going to change, now we will beat those Tommies so bad they will be begging to go back to England." Though joyful to finally see air support, the tension of the men could not be overcome by their celebration and jokes. They were gripped by apprehension, not knowing what was to come. There would surely be hard and deadly battles ahead of them, and survival was no safe bet.

The boys were standing around the vehicles, some chatting with their comrades and others alone, silently smoking cigarettes deep in self-thought. "Now that we have the Luftwaffe hunting the Tommies, I wonder if the counter attack has already started?" Kristian said to Gunny.

"Hey, maybe it has and they no longer need us. Wouldn't that be nice," Gunny said with and optimistic smile.

"No, my friend," Kristian said. "Even with the Luftwaffe, I think they're going to need every man that can pull a trigger. Did you already forget what we saw at the beach?"

"Oh no," Gunny said. "I definitely haven't forgotten that."

"Just keep that in your head," Kristian said.

"Shit is going to get bad."

"Mount up," the sergeant shouted, "were moving out."

Chapter Twenty-three

Minutes after the scouting team began to roll, a convoy

of vehicles began passing by in the opposite direction towards

the coast. The vehicles were perfectly camouflaged, looking like

moving bushes as they came down the road. The faces of the

men were very young and covered with dirt from their long

journey. Their column consisted of all kinds of vehicles, APC's,

radio vehicles, tractors with mounted infantry, anti-tank guns,

motorcycle gunners and command vehicles. The boys in the 12th

SS column shouted to the Army troops, "Hoo-rah, good luck,

comrades, and to victory." The Army soldiers shouted back,

"good luck to you," and others would jokingly say. "You're

going the wrong way."

The column again got underway. The further they got down the road the more vehicles they saw that had been knocked out by the enemy. Burned out rusty colored vehicles sitting where they were hit. Some were unrecognizable, the result of terrible explosions caused by Allied fighter bomber attacks. Loose ammunition, dead soldiers and bomb craters were all around. Kristian noticed that next to one of the bomb craters sat a knocked-out APC. The rear of the vehicle open, the legs and lower body of a soldier was sticking out. As Kristian's vehicle slowly passed by, he and Gunny could see that the soldier's upper body was completely burnt. "I hope a bullet killed that poor bastard before he burned to death," Kristian told Gunny.

As the column passed through a small town, Kristian saw the vehicles in front of him come to a quick stop and the men within them jumping out in search of cover. Kristian almost instinctively knew what that meant, a fighter bomber was barreling down upon them. Kristian and the other boys in the vehicle quickly grabbed their rifles and exited the vehicle as fast as possible and ran for cover. All of the men opened fire with their rifles as the fighter bombers swept down and strafed the column. Undamaged, the aircraft flew off into the sun and out of sight. As the men began to gather themselves and load back up into the vehicles, coming out of the sun were the two fighter bombers making another run on the column.

With their engines howling at high speed racing toward the column in a low-level attack, the aircraft opened fire on them. "Brrt, brrt, brrt," the salvo began ripping up the street, two vehicles and several men. The casualty count was one noncom, (noncommissioned officers) and three men killed, as well as one officer, one noncom and three men wounded. Kristian ran over to one of the wounded men. His arm had been blown off below the elbow and he was bleeding profusely. Kristian knew that if he didn't apply a tourniquet soon the boy would surely bleed to death. "Hey, buddy," Kristian said to the boy trying to calm him as he frantically struggled to take the belt off from the soldier's waste to use as a tourniquet. "You're going to be just fine. Let me just get this on your arm to stop the bleeding, then we will get you to an aid station. Looks like you're going home, pal."

Kristian and the other boys provided first aid to the wounded as best they could under the circumstances. Medical supplies were nearly non-existent with combat troops, due to shortages in almost everything at this point in the war. As Kristian worked on the wounded soldier, the platoon sergeant walked up and stood over them assessing the injuries the boy had. "Am I going to be okay?" the soldier asked Kristian, as his body shook in shock.

"Sure, you are," Kristian said to the boy in an attempt to reassure him and calm him down. Kristian looked up at the sergeant as if asking his opinion, and the sergeant's non-verbal reply was a light shaking of his head no, then sadly looking down and slowly walking away.

The men loaded the wounded men into the vehicles and left the dead to be recovered by support troops later. The severely injured were laid on the floor of the vehicles. The blood dripping on the floor made it slick and difficult to maneuver around inside the trucks. Kristian and Gunny sat with the injured boy that lay on the floor who had lost his arm. Kristian held the boy's remaining hand and continued to talk to the boy to keep him calm.

"What's your name?" Kristian said the boy.

"I'm Adam," he replied, wincing from the pain.

"Hi Adam, I'm Kristian and this is Gunny. Where are you from? Kristian asked,

trying to get the boy's mind off of the pain.

"I live on a farm, in Bavaria," Adam replied.

"When you think about home, what is the first thing you think about?" Kristian asked.

"I think of the animals," the boy said. "I know it sounds strange, but I enjoyed my chores and taking care of the animals. I also think of lying in the meadow, not a sound to be heard but the sound of the blowing wind. And the occasional 'moo' from a cow," the boy said jokingly and they all three chuckled.

"I think of my mom baking," Kristian told Adam. "It seemed she was always baking or cooking something; I don't know how she got anything else done. I didn't care back then though, I was just happy to enjoy her pies and cakes," Adam said with a light smile.

"How about you, Gunny?" Adam said.

"Well, the first thing that comes to mind is my little brother," Gunny said with a smile, chuckling to himself about his thoughts. "I remember, my brother and I were small boys still under 10 years of age. We climbed on the roof of the house and I told my brother that if he held on to each corner of a sheet and jumped off of the roof, he would float to the ground like a feather."

"Did he jump?" Adam said.

"Yeah, he jumped. He jumped off of the roof and hit the ground so hard, that he broke his leg." Kristian and Adam began laughing at Gunny's story. "I got in a lot of trouble for that," Gunny added, and the three continued to laugh.

"I've to close my eyes, I'm so tired," Adam said slowly, blinking his eyes a couple of times. Then the blinking stopped and Adam stared into the sky as his young hand lost his grip from Kristian's hand, falling to the floor.

Kristian and Gunny both continued to look at Adam, both in sorrow and in disbelief that he was gone. Just seconds before Adam was laughing and joking with them and in an instant the life in him slipped away.

"Well, he's not hurting anymore," Gunny said sadly.

"Yeah," Kristian said, "maybe in a way, he is better off. He wasn't going to make it anyway and if you're going to die it's better quicker than later."

"True, true," Gunny said shaking his head in agreement. "And he was happy, not a bad way to go," Gunny said, trying to convince both Kristian and himself that it was for the best. Kristian leaned over and closed Adams eyes with his fingers, then Kristian laid his jacket over Adam's lifeless body.

Kristian sat there silently staring at the jacket lying over Adam's body. Gunny looked at Kristian for a few seconds and became worried at what was on Kristian's mind that would put him that deep in thought.

"Hey," Gunny said to Kristian, giving his shoulder a nudge. "Are you okay? What's going on in that thick head of yours?"

Kristian turned his head to Gunny and looked at him with a playful semi-snarl. "Oh, I'm just thinking about Holly," Kristian said.

"How can you be thinking about sex now? Gunny said with an almost revolted expression. "There's something seriously wrong with you pal."

"I'm not thinking about sex you moron," Kristian said. "I'm worried for her safety. If everything is going to hell where we are, what the hell is it like where she is?"

"I'm sure she is fine," Gunny said. "She is far enough away from the coast for anything to be going on there. I'm sure it's as quiet and serene as it always is.

" You're probably right," Kristian said. "Have you two talked about if the invasion did come where you might meet up if things got bad?" Gunny said.

"No, we haven't," Kristian said with a worried look on his face.

"I didn't even think about that. I didn't think the invasion would even come or even be possible."

"Surprise, pal," Gunny said sarcastically, "it has, and it is. Is there any place you think she might go, where you would be able to find her?"

Kristian thought for a second then quickly perked up. "Belgium. She would go to Belgium, I'm sure of it," Kristian said.

"Well there you go," Gunny said. "See, there's nothing to worry about; you can meet her there."

The Canadians had been able to take St. Aubin on the HJ's left flank, but the British were unable to capture Lion-sur-Mer, denying them the ability to link up to combine forces and push further inland. There was a 5-kilometer gap between the two Allied forces, leaving an excellent opportunity for the Germans to make a successful counter attack, pushing them back to the coastline. The column was ordered to the west side of the Orne but had to cross the river at Caen. The city had been heavily bombarded by the Allies and the streets were covered in rubble from the buildings that had been decimated. Smoke and fire engulfed the city, it was as if anything that could burn was burning. This included the bodies of soldiers and civilians, men, women and children that were scattered across the landscape. The stench was overwhelming and it literally looked like hell.

The column, slowly made their way through the debris covered street. Occasionally the men would have to get out of the vehicles to remove obstacles, and bodies, they were unable to pass. At one of the unscheduled stops, the men dismounted from the vehicles and began clearing the street ahead of the convoy. As they worked surrounded by fires, smoke and mangled bodies, the soothing sound of Beethoven's 5th symphony could be heard being played flawlessly on piano. Not believing what they were hearing, the men stopped working and began walking to the sound of the piano. In the corner of a building that had all but collapsed, leaving only a small portion of a room still intact, a young SS soldier had discovered an undamaged piano and could not resist the opportunity to play.

All of the men, including the officers and noncoms stood silently watching as this young man performed magic with his fingers. For a moment they were taken away from the hell that they were in and transported to a place and time of peace and comfort. The men smiled as they rocked back and forth in rhythm with the song so eloquently played on the piano. As the song ended and the keys went quiet, the men stood there in silence for a moment with an afterglow expression on their faces from the joy received by the beautiful serenade. As if snapping back to reality, in unison the men broke out in applause praising the young pianist. "Alright men," the sergeant gruffly shouted. "Enough screwing around, back to work." The sergeant enjoyed the beauty of the song just as much as the men did, but he would not allow the sensitive side of his demeanor to be exposed in front of the men.

Chapter Twenty-Four

The Allies had taken the beachhead and were moving inland, but the advance slowed and they began to struggle near Cambes. The 12th SS had taken up positions there, and due to wooded areas and stone wall fences, the Allies had no idea where the Germans were. It was a perfect place to ambush the enemy. Kristian's *Kampfgruppe* (battle group) consisted of one tank battalion of 90 Mark IV tanks, three infantry battalions and artillery, plenty of firepower to bring a screeching stop to the Allied advance. Kristian and his platoon were still trying to fortify their firing positions when a Sherman tank rumbled out of the woods and onto a side road.

The platoon was spotted immediately and the turret of the tank turned and took direct aim at them. "Tank," Kristian shouted to his comrades. The boys quickly ran to the closest stone fence and jumped over, in an effort to hide them from the view of the tank gunner. The Sherman fired a round at the boys just as they jumped over the fence with the round hitting just short of the stone wall. Luckily, the round the tank fired was an anti-tank round and not an explosive round. Had it been the latter, it would have surely killed them all. "Follow me," Kristian told the other boys and began crawling along the fence line, away from the point where they had jumped over the fence. About fifty meters away the boys stopped crawling and sat on the ground leaning against the wall.

Kristian wanted to make sure that they were far enough away from the point where they came over the fence that if the tank kept firing at that location, the boys would be far enough away to avoid injury. The tank did not continue to fire at the boys, so they slowly raised up to look over the stone wall to see if the tank was heading toward them. A young HJ soldier, dug in near the Sherman, ran close to the tank and fired a *Panzerfaust* (anti-tank rocket) at point blank range. The ensuing explosion took out the tank, destroying it and rendering it useless, as well as killing the young soldier that fired the rocket. "That guy was one brave bastard or one stupid son of a bitch," Gunny said, shaking his head in disbelief.

The burning Sherman blocked the main intersection for the passage of any following tanks. The Panzer tanks hidden in camouflaged positions in the tree line, began to open fire on the enemy tanks that were detained behind the destroyed Sherman. One of the Panzer's rounds hit another Sherman, taking that tank as well and leaving it burning on the road further hindering the British advance. One of the Sherman's began returning fire at the Panzers with one of the rounds hitting the tree tops above one of the tanks. The trees fell on the center of one of the tanks, blocking its visibility and preventing the turret from turning, making it impossible to accurately return fire. The other Sherman's began to open fire as well with one of the rounds hitting the tracks of another Panzer, disabling it from maneuvering.

A third Panzer returned fire destroying another Sherman, then began moving forward to get a better position to fare upon the other Sherman tanks. As the Panzer crossed the field it slid sideways into one of the bomb craters created by the allied aerial bombardment. The tank was unable to pull itself out of the crater and the bottom of the tank was sticking up out of the crater, dangerously exposing it to enemy fire and rendering it useless. One of the Sherman's took aim at the helpless Panzer and fired a round into the belly of the tank. The round from the Sherman hit its target, entering the tank and exploding inside, blowing the tank commander out of the turret as if he was shot out of a cannon, followed by a pillar of fire from within the tank.

At the same time the gunner began to crawl out of the tank turret, the driver's hatch opened on the burning Panzer and both men exited the tank, their bodies engulfed in fire. Just seconds after the crew made it out of the burning wreckage their bodies fell to the ground charred, unrecognizable and lifeless. "Dear God," Gunny said with a look of both shock and horror on his face. "Those poor bastards."

"Yeah," Kristian said. "Kind of makes you glad you're in the infantry and not stuck in one of those metal coffins."

"Those guys think they got it better surrounded by all that armor, but they're just a bigger target that everyone and their mother has in their cross hairs," Gunny said.

"I'm with you pal," Kristian said. "This tunic isn't very thick but I feel a lot safer in it than I would in one of those things."

The Highlanders of the 3rd Canadian Army advanced into the orchards and were quickly cut down like wheat during harvest by the German ground troops, tank battalion and relentless artillery. Though the Canadians gave a brave and valiant effort to take the battlefield, the overwhelming German firepower forced them to withdraw back to the village of Authie. After the Canadians withdrew, Kristian and his squad were ordered to take a patrol down to the burning Sherman's to search for survivors that could be interrogated for information on Allied plans and positions. Kristian had taken point on the patrol and was about 25 meters in front of the rest of the men getting close to the knocked out Canadian tanks when the distinct whistling sound of artillery rounds began to rain down on the patrol.

Kristian quickly dove into a bomb crater that had been created by an earlier Allied bombardment to escape the deadly shrapnel from the exploding artillery shells. To Kristian's surprise, he discovered that the crater was already occupied by a Canadian soldier, just as surprised and startled as Kristian, on the other side of the crater. The Canadian was unarmed, but Kristian still had his rifle and quickly aimed it at the Canadian. Kristian tried to chamber a round into the rifle, but he was unable to. It was jammed, and was not able to chamber a round. The Canadian soldier quickly pulled his bayonet from his belt and Kristian just as quickly followed suite. Both men sat on opposite sides of the crater, bayonets in hand ready for mortal hand to hand combat.

Kristian and the Canadian continued to sit in the crater, staring each other down with their battle faces, both waiting for the other to make the first move as artillery shells exploded all around them. Kristian's adrenalin was rapidly pumping through

272

his veins and as he concentrated on the Canadian, he forgot all about the deadly artillery rounds exploding just meters away. As the two men calmed down and hesitantly lowered their bayonets, still keeping a watchful eye on each other. After a few tense minutes, the Canadian soldier stuck the point of his bayonet in the dirt, reached into his shirt pocket and pulled out a pack of cigarettes. The Canadian took a cigarette out of the pack and put it to his lips, then looked at Kristian with a curious look on his face.

The Canadian soldier shook his pack of cigarettes until one of the cigarettes stuck out of the opening of the pack and with a friendly smile leaned over to Kristian holding the pack at arm's length, offering Kristian a cigarette. Kristian, surprised at the Canadian's friendly offer, slowly and carefully reached out and took the cigarette accepting the Canadian's kind gesture. The Canadian pulled out his lighter, flipped the cap open and lit his cigarette and as the flame continued to burn held out his lighter to Kristian offering him a light. Kristian put the cigarette to his lips and while carefully watching the Canadian, reluctantly leaned into the lighter and lit his cigarette. Kristian leaned back against the wall of the crater and continued to watch the Canadian.

The Canadian soldier put his cigarette to his lips and took a deep drag and exhaled a cloud of smoke. "Ahh," the Canadian sighed with a smile and holding up his cigarette. "Good cigarette." Kristian took a drag of the cigarette and as he blew the pleasant and satisfying smoke out of his lungs, he could tell that the quality of the tobacco the Canadians had was much better quality than the Germans had. "Mmm, good," Kristian said with a smile. Both men enjoyed their cigarette and occasional one would speak to the other as if having a conversation, but the Canadian not knowing German and Kristian not knowing English, both of their efforts were unproductively one sided.

As suddenly as the artillery bombardment started, it stopped and the only thing that Kristian could hear was the ringing of his ears. Both the Canadian and Kristian waited a few minutes to make sure the artillery strike had truly ended before attempting to leave the safety of the bomb crater. Once they had determined the danger was over the two men shook hands with a

274

smile as if wishing each other luck to survive the nightmare they had been thrust into. Both men crawled to the top of the crater and looked over the edge making sure that there was no danger before making their run to safety. Kristian and the Canadian looked at each other one last time, gave each other a quick salute, crawled out of the crater and sprinted in opposite directions to their own army's held lines.

Kristian made it back to the German held lines where the rest of his patrol had gathered and regrouped.

"Hey, did I just see what I think I just saw?" Gunny said Kristian.

"What's that?" Kristian said.

"I could swear that I saw you and an enemy soldier crawl out of the same crater," Gunny said with a confused look on his face.

"You did," Kristian said, then started to walk away. Gunny grabbed the sleeve of Kristian's tunic, stopping him from walking away.

"You mean you were both in the same crater that whole time and you didn't kill him?' Gunny said.

"No, neither one of us had a weapon, so we had a cigarette instead," Kristian said, then again began to walk away.

Gunny, still confused and not understanding what the hell was going on, grabbed Kristian by the sleeve again. "What a minute," he said with a very curious expression on his face. "What do you mean, you had a cigarette? You both just sat there together and smoked cigarettes?"

"Pretty much," Kristian said. "Then we exchanged numbers and he invited me over for dinner after the war."

"What?" Gunny asked, even more bewildered than he was before. "Your shitting me, right? You got to be shitting me. Your shitting me, aren't you? Aren't you?" Gunny asked, standing there still baffled at what he had just heard. Kristian smiled at Gunny then turned and walked away. "Hey, hey, you're an asshole Ackmann," Gunny shouted. Kristian continued walking, chuckling to himself as he walked away.

Before Kristian could get away the platoon sergeant stopped by the squad's assigned area to check status and brief them of their new orders. "Ackmann, get back over here, I've some information I need you to hear," the sergeant said. Kristian walked back over to the squad and the sergeant began to brief the boys. "Okay, listen up," the sergeant ordered. "We are digging in here for the night, so settle in and make sure you have your firing positions ready and your fields of fire determined for each man. Tomorrow morning's briefing will be at 0500, squad leaders only, that's you Ackmann. The rest of you men, man your positions and keep your eyes open. The Tommies or Canadians could make a counterattack at any moment, so stay alert. That is all."

Chapter Twenty-Five

It was apparent that the cost of the day's attack was high for the HJ Division. The grounds of the Abby were littered with the wounded, the dying and the dead. The 2nd Battalion commander, along with most of the company commanders, had perished or were severely wounded by a well-placed artillery shell, leaving lower ranking and unexperienced officers in command of the remaining units. This would prove to create a dire situation for the HJ Division with being understrength in tanks, men and artillery. The loss of the combat-experienced officers could mean the demise of the entire division. With the loss of senior officers, rank had to quickly be adjusted to accommodate the situation. Lower ranking officers were promoted and non-coms were made lower ranking officers.

The following morning before briefing, Sergeant Dirks, now promoted to Platoon Leader, approached Kristian's squad position accompanied by two young replacements. "Allright, listen up," Dirks ordered. "You got two new men, Privates Karl Hanze and Art Schmidt." The two boys looked like they couldn't be over 16 and looked as if they were scared to death. "Ackmann, you are now Corporal and in charge of this squad, perhaps even the platoon if shit don't get better. Hanze, Schmidt," Dirks said, looking at the two new boys, "You stay right on Ackmann's ass. If he tells you to jump, don't waste time asking how high, you just jump. Got it?"

"Yes sir," the boys replied, a little surprised at the command they had been given.

"Good, it might be the only thing that keeps your asses alive."

Looking at Kristian, Dirks noticed that he didn't look like the normal happy go lucky Ackmann that he had always known. "Ackmann, come over here, I want to talk to you for a minute," Dirks ordered. Kristian stood up and walked over to Dirks and together walked out of ear range of the other men.

"All right, Kristian," Dirks said. "I've known you quite a while now and I can tell something is on your mind. I want you to spill it, before you take charge and lead these men. I need to know now."

"No sir," Kristian said. "I'm just a little worried about my girl."

"This is no time to be thinking about your sweetheart back home, so you better just get that crap out of your head. I need you clear-headed; if you keep thinking about that shit you are going to get you and your men killed, and we need every man we can get right now."

"She's here," Kristian told Dirks.

"What do you mean she's here? Where?"

Dirks asked, a little confused. "She lives in Falaise," Kristian said.

"A French girl?" Dirks said with a surprised look on his face.

"Yes," Kristian said.

"Well, aren't you a fast worker. I guess you don't fool around, but then again, I guess you do," Dirks said with a smile, attempting to lighten Kristian up with a little jocularity.

Kristian chuckled and smiled at Dirk's levity. "I met her in Belgium during training and later found out she was from Falaise. Then we got transferred here, it was like fate or something," Kristian told Dirks.

"What's her name?" Dirks said. "Holly," Kristian said. "Is she pretty?" Dirks said with an eyebrow flash. "Beautiful," Kristian said with a proud smile. "Well," Dirks said. "If you want to see her again you had better get her out of your head until then."

"Come on," Dirks told Kristian, putting his hand on Kristian's shoulder with a little pat and directing him to follow. "Let's get back to your squad, I need to give you a quick briefing. You and your men are going out on a patrol."

Dirks called the squad together around him and began giving them their orders of the day. "Men, do you see that church steeple on that hill over there?" Dirks said pointing at an old church at the top of a hill just on the edge of the horizon.

"Yes sir," the squad replied in unison.

"I want you men to go to that church and get someone up in that bell tower to get information on troop movements, manpower and equipment. This might be a little tricky; we believe that the church is already occupied by the Canadians and they're using it for the exact same reason."

Dirks looked at each of the boys faces in the squad. "You boys are brothers and you are going to have to look after each other like brothers. This is going to be dangerous and you are going to have to be extremely careful. If the enemy sees you coming they can pick you off one by one; they have the higher ground and you'll be easy targets with little cover to hide behind. If and when you to take the church, the enemy must not know that we have it because they will surely mount a counter attack

282

or just blow the shit out of it with artillery. We know we are outnumbered, outgunned and have no air support. We have got to have this intelligence so that we can get the upper hand and even out the playing field a little.

"It is extremely important that you accomplish this mission, the rest of the battalion is counting on you and this can be a turning point in the battle giving us the opportunity to push them back into the sea. Do you boys understand?"

"Yes sir," the boys said. "We will teach those Tommies and Canooks not to mess with the German Reich." Karl, one of the new replacements boldly stated, as he stuck out his chest with pride and determination.

"Calm down there, big fella," Dirks said wisely, dealing out a good piece of advice. "Don't underestimate those boys, they're going to put up a hell of a fight and if you don't keep your shit together, you won't be going home to eat your momma's cookies anymore,"

Kristian made sure that his men checked their gear and loaded up with as much ammunition as they could carry, then the patrol moved out to take their objective. "Okay guys," Kristian said to the squads." Stay in single file, five to ten meters apart; we don't want one grenade taking out half of the squad. Keep your eyes open and your mouths shut. Keep your asses down, you're not taking a stroll through the park, and those men aren't the choir welcoming you to church on Sunday. Got it?" All the boys nodded their heads, letting Kristian know that they understood exactly what they were going into. "Okay, let's go," Kristian told the boys waving them to follow. "Remember stay down and pay attention to the orders that I give you."

The patrol slowly and carefully made their way to the church using every bush, tree and rock they could find to conceal them along the way. About 100 meters away from the church the patrol gathered to listen to Kristian's instructions for the assault. Kristian pointed at two of the squad members, Michael and Fritz. "I want you two to take the lead on the assault. I want you two leapfrogging every ten meters covering each other as you move forward. Once you both reach the church you'll provide cover for the rest of the squad to move forward. Once the squad reaches the church, Michael and Fritz will kick in the door and we will go room to room clearing each one, working our way up to the bell tower. Karl and Art, you stick with me. Everyone understand?" The boys each gave Kristian a thumbs up letting him know the mission was clear.

Michael and Fritz readied themselves for their sprint toward the church. Once Michael determined the coast was clear he stood up and ran about ten meters toward the church then knelt down with rifle ready to cover Fritz as he ran forward. Fritz stood up and sprinted towards the church. Just as he passed Michael a shot rang out from the bell tower of the church. The round from the Canadian's rifle pierced the front of Fritz's helmet, went through his head and exited the rear of his helmet. Fritz's body went limp and fell in the dirt creating a small dust cloud, his life taken even before hitting the ground. Michael raised the barrel of his rifle trying to get a bead on the sniper in the tower but could not see him in the shadows. Kristian then pointed at Walter, another member of the squad and waved him forward to take Fritz's place.

Walter stood up and began running as fast as he could toward the church and just as he ran past Fritz's body another shot rang out from the bell tower, this time missing its target. Walter took a knee, then aimed up at the bell tower to cover Michael as he ran to the church. Michael reached the church without a shot being fired from the sniper and stood outside the front door giving cover to Walter as he ran forward to join him. Michael looked around the front of the church and in the windows but saw no threat to the squad, so he waved Kristian and the rest of the men forward. The remaining members of the squad stood up and made a mad dash toward the church hoping that their numbers and speed would cause the sniper to miss his target in confusion.

Fifty meters away from the church, riflemen accompanied by machine-gun fire were now coming from the bell tower spraying men with a hail storm of bullets. Two more members of the squad were killed during the assault leaving only 7 men to take the building. Once the men were in place and ready to enter and sweep the church, Michael and Walter kicked in the door then rushed in quickly followed by the rest of the squad. Kristian and the rest of his teams' hearts were pounding as adrenalin pumped through their veins expecting a point-blank firefight accompanied with brutal hand to hand combat, but to almost their dismay found no one in the room.

Taking a moment to catch their breaths and mentally regroup, they looked at each other in disbelief of finding no one inside. The sound of a man running came from upstairs and the squad snapped to and prepared themselves once again for the fight. Slowly the team began walking up the stairway, weapons pointing up to the second floor ready to shoot anyone exposing themselves to fire. Reaching the second floor there were two doors and another narrow stairway to the bell tower. "You two men take the door to the left," Kristian told two of the boys. "And you two take the door on the right. At the count of three enter the rooms at the same time and sweep them for the enemy. Us three will cover for you both." The boys got close to the doors, ready to rush in.

"Ready?" Kristian said in a heavy whisper and the boys gave him a thumbs up. Kristian began the count for the assault in a whisper and raising a finger for each number said, "one, two, three." Both teams rushed in their rooms ready for a fight, but once again found no one there. The only place left was the bell tower, and the only way up was a narrow stairway that only one man at a time could fit on. The boys in the squad all looked at each other as if asking, who is going to volunteer to go up those stairs? Michael held up his hand and slowly began ascending the stairway. At the top was a wood ceiling door to the entrance of the bell tower and Michael quickly pushed it open.

As the ceiling door swung open, Michael began to run up the last few stairs to enter the bell tower and was immediately met with a burst of machine-gun fire. Several rounds ripped through the brave young boy's chest, exploding out of his back and causing him to fall out of the bell tower and down the stairway to the floor below. The rest of the squad pointed their rifles and MP 40 machine-guns at the ceiling and into the bell tower, opening up with everything they had. Hundreds of rounds went through the ceiling into the bell tower assuring no one would survive. Once the boys stopped firing, they stood and listened for movement, but heard nothing. Kristian pulled a grenade from his belt and gave the other boys a smile, then pulled the pin and threw the grenade up into the tower for good measure.

Chapter Twenty-Six

The next day when the church had been taken, Kristian and his squad were relieved and brought back to the rear of the lines to replace the men they had lost. Kristian and the remaining survivors of the assault were awarded the Iron Cross 2nd Class medal for bravery in combat. This medal was a rite of passage for a German soldier that designated him as a true and tested combat soldier. Now the young SS men no longer would be looked down upon as newbies, untested in battle. They could proudly display the medal's ribbon on their tunic, showing all other soldiers that they were now hardened veterans.

London had been getting hammered by Hitler's V-1 flying bomb and it was imperative that the British and Canadians capture the bridgeheads to get access to the launching sites. The V-1's had to be stopped; thousands of British citizens were being annihilated by what Hitler called his Wonder Weapon. Around Cheux the fighting was desperate, but for the moment units of the 12th SS HJ Division were holding the British and Canadians from advancing. Kristian and his newly decorated comrades were quickly transported back to the front in an effort to reinforce the troops now engaged in a pitched battle with the Allies. The transport truck carrying Kristian and his squad was barreling down the road as fast as it could safely maneuver the unpaved roads in an effort to reach the front as soon as possible.

The boys in the back of the truck were bounced around and thrown into each other with every pothole in the road. It was as if the driver was intentionally hitting every one of them he could find. "Son of a bitch," Gunny shouted to be heard over the loud moan of the truck engine. "What kind of maniac is driving this thing. He is going to have us killed before we even get to the front." Kristian and the other boys smiled and chuckled at Gunny's remark as they continued to be bounced around the back of the vehicle.

"If we get killed, it'll save us from having to eat those damn field rations we get," Michael shouted, continuing the humorous complaining that is so common between soldiers that share the same hardships.

"Be grateful you get those," Kristian shouted. "You might not get anything to eat for days soon."

The transport truck pulled up in front of a small building that the remaining officers of the HJ Division had appropriated for a command center and came to a screeching halt, throwing all of the boys forward against the cab of the truck. Explosions and small arms fire could be heard from about a kilometer away, welcoming the boys back to the front. "All right boys," the truck driver shouted out of the cab window. "Get your butts out quick so I can get the hell out of here." The boys began jumping out of the back of the truck one by one and before the last man could jump down out of the truck, the driver began pulling away causing the boy to fall to the ground.

"Hey asshole," Gunny shouted at the driver.

"You chicken shit, you didn't even have the guts to stick around until we all got out. What a coward."

"He'll get his in the end," Kristian told Gunny. "They always do,"

Kristian helped the young boy who fell out of the truck to his feet and gave him a look over to make sure he was alright. The boy was one of the new replacements, straight from the training camp. "You'll be okay," Kristian told the boy. "Too bad you didn't break your arm."

"What?' The boy said with a confused look on his face, wondering why Kristian would think breaking his arm would be a good thing. "Hey, if you broke your arm you could get the hell out of here and not have to go out there and get shot at." "I don't want to go back, I want to go to the front and fight," the boy said as if boasting his bravery. "What's your name kid?" Kristian said the boy.

"My name is Adam," he said.

"Listen up Adam," Kristian said authoritatively. "We've been up there, there's nothing glorious about war. The only thing you're going to find out there is death."

Adam looked at Kristian with both disappointment and disbelief on his face, then gruffly began brushing the dirt from the road off of his uniform. Kristian turned to the other boys in the squad and began to give them orders. "Okay guys we're going to...."

"Hey you little urchins, you made it back just in time," Dirks said interrupting, Kristian as he came out of the door of the command building.

The boys in the squad turned around to see Dirks with smiles on their faces. Dirks was a soldier's soldier and the boys had great respect for him; they always felt a little safer when he was around. Dirks loved his boys as well, and though he never showed it, it always tore him up inside when something would happen to one of them.

"Okay boys, listen up," Dirks ordered. "We're heading up to the front right now, there's a tank battalion just on the other side of the tree line that needs infantry support. We're extremely undermanned and each one of you is going to have to do the duty of two soldiers. We're outnumbered in both tanks and men, but we cannot let them advance anymore inland. We are expecting the Tommies and Canadians to mount an attack at any moment. They've been trying to soften up our lines with artillery and sporadic fire from tanks and ground troops. This is going to be no picnic boys. All hell is about to break loose, and you have to be at the top of your game.

"We are supporting the second platoon of the 21st Panzer Division and we are going to be spread pretty thin out there," Dirks continued. "I'm going to break you up into two-man teams, two men on either side of the tanks, keeping a 30 to 40-meter distance. If they get hit

294

with a tank round, I don't want it taking out one of you as well. Keep your asses down in the dirt, you're not to move unless there's an infantry assault and you have to defend the tanks. I don't want to lose any of you little turds without a damn good reason. We clear?"

"Yes sir," the squad said.

"Okay boys, follow me and I'll show you to your positions," Dirks ordered. The boys followed Dirks stretched out in a line behind him. There was light chit chat and little taunts and teases between the boys along the way, typical behavior of most soldiers about to stare death in the face.

At the front Dirks split the boys up in twos trying to pair the most experienced boys with the least. Kristian was pared with young, gung-ho Adam and wasn't really thrilled about it, but he could remember when he was exactly like young Adam and what a slap in the face it was when he got a dose of reality. Kristian made up his mind to take Adam under his wing to teach him how to stay alive, and to make his baptism of fire as painless as possible. "Listen kid," he told Adam. "Remember, keep your ass down just like Dirks told you and if I tell you to run, get the hell out of here as fast as you can. And no hero crap, this isn't a movie. You screw around here and you'll get your ass killed, probably taking me with you and I sure as hell don't want that. You do anything stupid, I'll shoot you myself."

All was quiet except for an occasional irritation round the Brits would fire at them to keep their nerves on edge, then the faint sound of tank engines and the squeaking of track rotating on the tanks began to be heard from the tree line across the field. "Here the bastards come," Kristian told Adam. "Get ready and remember to do what you were told and keep…your…ass…down!" "Don't worry about me," Adam said with a smart assed tone and a snarl. "I can take care of myself." Kristian rolled his eyes in disbelief at Adam's arrogance and naivety, then readied himself for the coming battle. American Sherman tanks and British Cromwell Mk IV tanks accompanied by infantry troops began pouring out of the tree line in overwhelming numbers and began to open fire on the German lines.

Explosive rounds and anti-tank rounds fired by the British tanks were exploding all around Kristian and Adam, and above their heads were the constant sound of bullets whizzing by, fired from the rifles and machine-guns of the attacking Allied infantry soldiers. Adam started to panic, nervously fidgeting and breathing as if he were about to hyperventilate. Kristian saw Adam acting as if he was about to bolt like a startled horse from a stable and became worried about what this foolish young boy might do. Adam pushed himself up by his arms in an attempt to get to his feet and run to safety, but Kristian quickly grabbed the sleeve of Adam's tunic and pulled him back to the ground. "What in the hell do you think you're doing, you idiot?" Kristian shouted, mad as hell at Adam's cowardly behavior.

Kristian slapped Adam on his helmet then pointed at the British soldiers coming toward them. "You better focus on them, dumbass, or they're going to kill your stupid ass," Kristian warned Adam. Kristian's actions jolted Adam's psychological state back together, mentally regrouping him so that he could pull himself together enough to tackle the job at hand. "Don't fire until they get closer," Kristian told Adam. "One shot, one kill. We don't have any ammo to spare, so make every shot count, got it?" Adam shook his head yes letting Kristian know that he fully understood the situation, accompanied with a look on his face as to apologize for his shameful behavior.

Kristian gave Adam a quick pat on his shoulder and smiled. "It's okay kid, we all get shook up now and then." Adam smiled in gratitude then turned and took aim at an approaching enemy soldier, waiting to make sure that he could make a clean kill. The Panzer tank on Kristian's right was hit by an anti-tank round and exploded, shooting fire out of the open driver's hatch and turret hatch. The driver crawled out of the hatch on fire and quickly succumb to the flames. The tank commander jumped out of the turret but forgot to take off his headset before jumping. The cord wrapped around the tank commander's neck, hanging him from the turret and slowly choking him to death.

Kristian stood up in the midst of the chaos and deadly gun fire and sprinted to the tank in an attempt to save the slowly dying tank commander. Kristian crawled up the side of the tank and untangled the cord from the man's neck. "Thank you," the commander said rubbing his neck, then he jumped off of the tank and ran for safety. Kristian looked over at Adam to make sure that he was okay. Adam was standing up pointing his rifle at a British soldier fully exposed to enemy fire. "Get down dumbass," Kristian shouted. As those words were coming out of Kristian's mouth, Adam's chest exploded, hit by a 50 caliber round fired from a Sherman tank.

Adam's body was blown back two meters from the velocity of the round that had ripped through his body, and fell to the ground. Kristian stood there frozen for a moment on the tank in shock from what he had just seen. Another 50 calibers round hit the turret right next to Kristian, throwing a small piece of shrapnel at him, grazing his face on his right cheek. Kristian instinctively put his hand to his face, touching his cheek then looked at his hand. He saw that his hand had blood on it and immediately jumped off of the tank. When he hit the ground, he felt excruciating pain from his right ankle. He tried to run but fell to the ground holding his ankle, reeling in pain.

Chapter Twenty-Seven

Dirks saw Kristian hopping back from the front, jumping on his right foot and favoring his left, exposed and still close enough to be picked off by the enemy. Dirks ran to Kristian and put Kristian's right arm over his shoulders to get him out of the range of fire as quickly as possible. "Where are you hit?" Dirks said. "Is it bad?"

"No, not too bad," Kristian said. "No. I know you're not going to believe this, but I think I sprained my ankle."

"Sprained your ankle?" Dirks said. Not only asking Kristian, but himself as well, still not believing what he was hearing. Kristian and Dirks continued to

300

talk and as they step in time, quickly hopping away from the death fields and flying bullets as fast as they could.

"You're a lucky bastard," Dirk said with a smile.

"Why in the hell would you think this is lucky?" Kristian said, not quite understanding Dirks reasoning.

"They will send you back to Falaise for a couple of days to recover, thanks to that lucky foot."

Kristian thought about it for a few seconds, a bit confused, then suddenly perked up with a smile on his face realizing what that meant. He would get to see Holly, at least for a little while. Kristian made it to the German medical unit to find it in utter chaos. There were bodies, parts of bodies and wounded everywhere. Medical supplies were nearly non-existent and there was nothing to ease the pain of the wounded soldiers. Soldiers were screaming. "Doctor, doctor, over here, over here please I need help." Younger soldiers heartbreakingly screaming for their mothers. "Mama, Mama, help me please mama, where are you?" What few medics and doctors available were running from wounded soldier to wounded soldier, in a fruitless attempt to save as many lives as possible.

Kristian sat in the grass surrounded by moaning wounded men, gently rubbing his ankle. One of the field surgeons, his white smock splattered with the blood knelt down to examine one of the men lying next to Kristian and began to look over his patient. Kristian watched the doctor as he performed his examination with a bit of curiosity, fascinated with the doctor's dedication to the men. The doctor looked away from the injured man and at Kristian noticing that he was watching him. "What's wrong with you?" the doctor asked Kristian with a rushed tone in his voice, as his hands patrolled the wounds of the soldier.

"I think I sprained my ankle," Kristian told the doctor as he began to stand.

The doctor looked at Kristian and rolled his eyes. "OK, let me take a look, stand on the leg and let's see what you've got." Kristian slowly began to apply pressure by standing on his leg and suddenly began to wince in pain. "Well, it looks like you're no good to us up here for a few days," he told Kristian, not happy about taking another desperately needed soldier from the

302

battlefield. "Get on that truck," the doctor said pointing to a truck loaded with wounded men, so crowded some men were stacked on top of the wounded that were unconscious. "That truck is headed back to Falaise. Rest there for a few days then get your ass back to the front as soon as possible. We need every man we can get."

Kristian slowly hopped over to the truck and found a small spot at the back of the truck where he could sit, trying carefully not to step on any of the wounded. The driver of the truck walked up to the back of the truck where Kristian was sitting.

"Well," the driver said looking surprised. "We actually have one going back that can still sit up. You're one of the lucky ones. The old man upstairs must like you," the driver said smiling at Kristian, then he walked away to get in the cab of the truck.

Kristian looked around at the other wounded boys in the truck. "Boy, I sure as hell am lucky."

"Damn lucky," he said shaking his head, grateful that he wasn't bleeding to death in the back of a truck, surrounded by other dying men.

The driver fired up the engine of the truck and the sound of the pistons firing began to drown out the painful moans of the men. With a sudden jerk of the truck, the driver began to pull away. Kristian had to quickly brace himself from the sudden jolt with his injured leg and began to reel in pain. One of the wounded soldiers lying below Kristian on the floor of the truck, with great effort raised his arm to grasp Kristian's hand. The young boy had a white blood-soaked cloth covering one eye as well as being wrapped around his head. The boy had also had a bullet pass through his shoulder and another through the thigh of the leg. Kristian grabbed the boy's hand and held it firmly and with a light shake said, "You're going to be all right kid." With a tired look the boy smiled back at Kristian, then closed his eyes.

Once in Falaise the truck stopped at a large white building that was being used as a makeshift hospital, whose sole purpose was to send home the boys they couldn't fix and fix the ones that they could to get them quickly back to the front. One of the doctors examined Kristian and determined that it would be best for him to stay off of his feet for a few days. Kristian was given the duty of visiting the wounded men and talking to them as they waited to be transported back to Germany. "We don't have a bunk for you to sleep on," the doctor told Kristian. "The cots are for the wounded. We can spare a blanket for you, so you'll have to find yourself a spot on the floor somewhere to sleep. Stay out of the way and help when needed; there are a lot of wounded boys that come through here so we can use every available hand."

Kristian walked over to a pile of blankets and grabbed the one on top. The blanket smelled of blood, dirt and sweat, but at this point he didn't care. He was exhausted, and as long as it would keep him warm during the night, that was all that mattered. At the back of the room there was a spot in the corner that was unoccupied and just big enough for Kristian to lay comfortably, so he quickly walked over and claimed the spot before it was given to another soldier. He laid down on the vacant spot and covered himself with the blanket, grateful for the opportunity to get a little sleep. Kristian lay his head on the wood floor and began staring at the ceiling, not at any certain object, just staring deep in thought.

As Kristian lay there with the moaning of the wounded in the background, he began to think of the soft moaning sounds Holly made when they kissed passionately. He began to get excited about getting the opportunity to see Holly and wondered to himself how he might get away from the hospital. As Kristian's mind ran scenarios through his head of ways to sneak away from there to see her, he slowly faded into sleep dreaming of the girl he longed to see. Kristian dreamed that Holly was standing on the wall of Falaise castle in a flowing white gown being delicately blown by the wind on a bright moonlit night as she stared out into the wilderness beyond the walls. Kristian watched as Holly slowly leaned forward until she fell like a domino off of the wall and out of his sight.

Kristian ran to the wall and looked down at the ground below expecting to see her lifeless body amid the rocks at the base of the castle wall, but only found a white dove flying over the treetops, the snow-white dove flying further and further away, then fading slowly into the fire-colored sun setting on the

306

horizon. The sound of loud moaning from one of the wounded soldiers pulled Kristian back from the serenity of his dream to the hell of reality. The moaning came from a young wounded boy lying close to him. The boy was regular army and had the misfortune of losing both of his arms from just above his elbows. Kristian pulled his blanket off and crawled over to the young soldier in an effort to help ease his pain anyway that he could.

Kristian got to the boy and put his hand gently on the boy's chest, "Is there anything I can do to help you buddy?"

"I'm afraid," the boy told Kristian as tears rolled down his face shaking from the pain.

"Don't worry kid," Kristian said to the boy patting him in reassurance on his chest. "You're going to be just fine. These guys will stitch you up and you'll be on your way home before you know it."

"Will you read me something from the bible?" the boy said.

"Sure, I guess," Kristian said, a little surprised from the request.

"I have a Bible in my tunic pocket, would you please get it and read me something from it?"

"Sure buddy," Kristian said, more than willing to do anything the wounded boy said.

He reached into the boy's tunic pocket and pulled out a small and very worn Bible that looked as if it itself had been in battle. Krystian flipped through the pages of the bible. "What is it you want me to read to you?"

"Just pick anything, it doesn't matter, just read me something," the boy said as if in desperation.

"Okay, uh let's see," Kristian said as he flipped through the Bible to select a page picked at random. "Let's see. It says here in (Deuteronomy 31:6) "Be strong and courageous. Do not be afraid or terrified because of them, for the LORD your God goes with you; he'll never leave you nor forsake you." Kristian raised his eyebrows, surprised at the significance of the randomly chosen verse.

"Wow," What are the odds of that happening; it sounds just like what you needed."

"It always is," the boy said. "All of the answers are in there, and you usually find them when you need them most."

"Do you really believe all of that superstition stuff?" Kristian said, clearly having doubt about believing in some God you couldn't see or hear. "What do you think about hell?" the boy said. "Sounds like a pretty damn bad place to be."

"Until you learn more about it, look at it this way," the boy told Kristian. "If you believe in God and then you die, and you find out there's no hell, you have lost nothing. But, if you don't believe in God and die and there's a hell, you're pretty much screwed."

Kristian thought about it for a second, pondering the boy's logic. "Well, I guess if you look at it that way, it would be the safer bet," Kristian admitted. "Okay," he said. "How do I become a Christian?"

"Well," the boy said. "I think you're supposed to be baptized, but in a case like this I think you can just say, 'I accept Jesus as my Lord and Savior.'"

"That's it, sounds pretty painless," Kristian said with a smile. "How do I say it again?"

"I accept Jesus as my Lord and Savior," the boy said.

"Okay," Kristian said, taking a breath then holding up his right hand for the oath. "I accept Jesus as my Lord and Savior," Kristian said looking as if he was proud of some great accomplishment.

"I don't think you have to raise your hand when you say it," the boy said. "But, it is a nice touch; he might like it."

Chapter Twenty-Eight

At the first opportunity, Kristian decided to quietly leave the make shift field hospital, determined to see Holly again. Holly's home was less than one kilometer away and normally the walk would not be that difficult, but Kristian's ankle created a problem. How to get from the hospital to Holly's house, without having to collapse reeling in pain from the walk when he got there. Kristian looked around the hospital for an available crutch or any other object he could use to aid him to walk on his bad leg as he made his way to the door of the building. Shoved to the side into a corner of the room, was a cane next to the body of a dead British officer. Kristian walked over to the dead man and curiously began looking him over.

The officer was a middle-aged man with graying black hair and a face that was pleasant and inviting, like someone you would want to have as a friend. Kristian stood next to him and looked over his face, trying to learn every character and line on it. Kristian thought to himself that if he saw the British officer in the sights of his rifle he surely would have killed him without hesitation, but being this close to this dead brave man-made Kristian very sad, thinking of the men that he had killed on the battle field. Were they kind and loving fathers? Were they dedicated husbands or a mother's promising son that was everything to her? These thoughts weighed heavy on Kristian's mind and for the first time he experienced sympathy for his enemy.

Kristian put his hand on the British officer's chest then closed his eyes and began to pray quietly so the other soldiers could not hear him. "God. I'm not sure if you are real or not, but I kind of hope that you are. This man looks like a good man and clearly, he was a brave man. I hope you allow soldiers to come to heaven; I've lost a lot of good friends and I hope that maybe one day I'll get to see them again. I know soldiers have to do a lot of bad shit, but we don't have much of a choice, being that it's them or us, and I hope you can keep that in consideration. I'm not sure that I'm doing this praying stuff right, but I sure hope you hear me out. Anyway, thanks God…and uh…Jesus too."

"That's a funny way to pray, but I don't think that God would care," a woman's voice said from behind Kristian. Hearing the woman's unexpected comment coming from behind him surprised and embarrassed Kristian, but he noticed that the voice was vaguely familiar. Kristian turned around to face the woman and make a joke about praying but was again surprised to see that the voice came from Holly. She looked exhausted and her baby blue dress was covered with the blood of wounded and dying soldiers, but she still could work up the energy to give Kristian a loving smile. Kristian's eyes drew open wide and the expression on his face went from the bowels of solemnness to the blissfulness of pure delight at seeing Holly once again.

Kristian and Holly both lunged at each other, wrapping their arms around one another and kissing ferociously as if to devour each other. The large room filled with men moaning in agony and pain became silent; all of the eyes of the wounded men were joyfully upon Kristian and Holly. The two young lovers finally noticed the strange silence and looked around the room try to find the reason, then found that every soldier was staring at them with smiles from ear to ear. "Kiss her again," one of the soldiers shouted. Kristian and Holly looked at each other smiling at the attention that they had attracted. "Yeah, kiss her again," another soldier shouted. Then, the rest of the soldiers jumped in.

Kristian smiled at Holly, then went in for the kill. Kristian put his arm around Holly's waist and pulled her to him with his right hand and grabbed a hand full of hair and gave it a light pull then, bent her back and began to kiss her passionately.

"Woo hoo," one of the soldiers shouted. "Ho ho yeah," another yelled as if they were home with the boys watching an old stag film. Kristian pulled Holly back up and relieved her from his tight embrace. "Okay," Kristian shouted to the wounded, ribbing the men. "Shows over, back to the moaning."

"Boo," an anonymous soldier shouted.

314

Kristian looked at Holly with a smile and little chuckle. "Let's get out of here" He grabbed Holly's hand and began to lead her out of the building.

They left the hospital and walked around the corner of the building where several trucks were parked that were used to carry the wounded from battle at the front. There were two rows of trucks, four in each row. Kristian and Holly went in between two of the trucks and walked to the center of the parked vehicles. Holly leaned back on the hood of one of the parked trucks and Kristian stood there for a second, silently staring at her young beautiful face and glistening brown eyes. "I want to make love to you so bad, I can hardly take it," Kristian told Holly with a look of pain on his face.

"I want you too," Holly confessed with a regretful sigh.

Kristian looked into Holly's eyes, his desire for her growing until finally reaching the blowing point of uncontrollable carnal desire. Kristian put his strong hands around Holly's waist and pulled her up and roughly turned her over face down of the hood of the truck. Kristian's sudden actions both frightened and excited Holly; the feeling of being man-handled felt sexually appealing somehow. Not rough and painful, just enough firmness to reinforce the fact that she was being made love to by a man. Kristian pulled Holly's dress just up above her hips and her panties down with one hand and holding her down against the hood of the truck with the other.

Holly tried to put up a fight, wrestling with Kristian to keep her dress down. Though in fear from the possible embarrassment of being discovered by someone at any moment, she also found it exciting and somehow enticing being desirably dirty sexually. No sooner had Holly's protest started, it ended suddenly when Kristian slid inside of her. Holly gasped for a breath of air, eyes wide open, shocked at Kristian's quick penetration and the utter bliss that she was experiencing. Kristian grabbed Holly's hips and forcefully thrust his hips against Holly's ass repeatedly, sounding as if being spanked and forcing his lust as deep inside her as he could.

Holly could not believe the feelings that she was experiencing; the feel of Kristian's strong masculine hands firmly holding her was heavenly. The feeling of the danger of being discovered was exhilarating and just added to the amazing sensations she was experiencing. As Kristian continued to forcefully thrust deep into her, he grabbed a handful of Holly's long brown hair and pulled it back toward him close enough to him that he could see her face. Kristian began thrusting harder and faster and between the feeling of both Kristian's thrusts, the · pulling of her hair and the danger of being discovered it was almost much more than Holly could take.

She began to moan in pleasure, louder and louder as the care for discovery slipped away from her consciousness. Holly was just on the edge of the best orgasm her young life had yet to have when Kristian reached up and firmly grasped Holly's breast and gently squeezed. The feeling of his strong masculine hand added to the pleasure she was experiencing, pushing her over the mountain and into the valley of ecstasy. As Holly peaked, Kristian exploded and Holly could feel the warmth coming in her, adding to the unbelievable pleasure she was experiencing. Kristian collapsed on top of Holly panting, trying to catch his breath. "Get up, you idiot before someone sees us," Holly demanded with a growl and an elbow into Kristian's ribs.

Rattled by the sharpness of Holly's request, Kristian quickly raised himself, freeing her to get herself back together and properly presentable.

"I can't believe you did that," Holly said with an angry look on her face as she struggled to get her dress down and over her petite hips. "I... I...," Kristian stammered trying to think of something to justify his animal behavior.

"It's okay though," Holly said with a smile, hopping lightly with giddiness. "I liked it," Kristian's face lit up, knowing that Holly enjoyed their little erotic interlude. *I'm definitely going to do this again*, Kristian said to himself as he thought about the amazing experience that they had together, and the pleasure it had brought them.

Holly grabbed Kristian by the hand and led him out of their secluded hideaway the parked trucks had provided and back to the hospital so she could return to helping the wounded. As they began to go around the corner to the front of the building, Kristian abruptly stopped walking and jerked Holly's arm, pulling her back to him. "Where are you going?" Kristian said, confused as to why Holly would go back inside the building so quickly.

"I've to go back; they need me," Holly told Kristian with a frown on her face. "They will be okay without you for a while," Kristian said in an attempt to convince her to stay with him.

"I love you Kristian and there's nothing I would love more than to get the chance to spend time with you, but those horribly wounded boys inside need me.

As those words were coming out of Holly's mouth, three transport trucks came quickly down the road and made a sudden halt in front of the hospital building. A gruff, scruffy and battle-weary middle-aged sergeant opened the cab door of the leading truck and stood commandingly up in the door well. "Every man who can carry a gun get your ass in the trucks, we're going to the front.

"Shit," Kristian said not pleased with the prospect of going back to the front, just in order to be used as cannon fodder for retreating army. "Well, I guess that settles that," Kristian said. "I'm going back and you're going in."

He silently looked deep into Holly's deceivingly innocent looking eyes for a moment, then bent down and softly, but passionately, kissed her lips. Holly began to cry in fear for Kristian's life; she knew the danger Kristian was going back to. But she also knew that neither one of them had any choice in the matter. Holly looked at Kristian and bravely smiled. "Don't worry," Holly said as she pulled his hand and held it against his child's mother's belly. "We will be waiting for you."

Kristian smiled, both proud and happy, then gave Holly one last passionate kiss goodbye. "I'll be back soon," Kristian said.

He then reluctantly pulled away from Holly's wanted embrace and walked toward the waiting supply trucks, repeatedly looking back at her as he walked away. Kristian climbed into the back of the truck with the other men and sat down next to the tailgate. Kristian and Holly continued to quietly gaze at each other, engraving the image of this moment into memory. The trucks began starting their engines, then slowly pulled away, beginning their journey back to dangers of the front. Holly stood outside the hospital and watched as the trucks drove away and out of view, trying to keep her composure while anguishing silently inside. Holly knew that the chance of them ever seeing one another again was slim at best.

Chapter Twenty-Nine

The Canadians broke through the lines of Germany's

85th Division, but Kristian and the 12th SS Panzer managed to

stop their advance. The 12th SS was down to only 11 tanks, a

dozen 88mm anti-tank guns and 300 infantrymen. The German

defense of Caen lasted until July 20th, when southern districts

were taken by the British and Canadian soldiers. The Germans

fought ferociously to hold Caen, but were overwhelmed by the

sheer number of men, machines and weapons that the Allies

could send into the battle. Kristian and his platoon were

patrolling on the western edge of the town of Caen in an attempt

to find any wounded that had been left behind, or German troops that had not been informed that they were ordered to pull all units out of Caen.

Heavy machine-gun fire opened up on the platoon and all of the men dove for cover as the British were attacking in great masses of infantry and tanks. Kristian was taking cover behind the rubble of a building, occasionally poking his head up above the debris in order to assess the situation. "Kristian," Karl one of the replacements in Kristian's platoon shouted, "What the hell do we do?"

"We fight as long as long as we can, then we get the hell out of here," Kristian shouted to Karl. But Kristian knew that they could not hold their positions long; the overwhelming numbers of the British forces would soon overtake them.

Kristian and his platoon fought valiantly and, in the process, lost many men. By the time the survivors tried to pull back, they realized that they were surrounded and that there was little chance of escape. Kristian attempted to retreat out of the town as fast as he could under the continuous fire from British machine-guns. He made it out of the range of small weapons fire, but others who tried to do the same failed. When British small arms fire stopped, the artillery bombardment began.

Artillery units from both the German and British sides began heavily shelling the entire area, with Kristian and the remaining boys from his platoon in the middle of the bombardment. Shells were falling two or three meters away from him with splinters of wood, rubble from exploding building and shrapnel from the artillery flying everywhere. Kristian and the rest of the men crawled on their stomachs, occasionally getting up on hands and knees to see if it was safe to continue their escape.

When the artillery bombardment ended, the British infantry renewed their attack with intense small-arms fire, and Kristian's hopes began to dwindle. The advancing British passed five or six paces away without noticing Kristian hiding in the high corn. Kristian's feet and elbows were in agony and his throat was parched from the lack of fresh water. As Kristian continued with his effort to escape capture, the corn field ended and he had to cross an open field. In between he and the field lay a road with wounded British soldiers walking back to their lines, passing within ten meters of Kristian without seeing him.

Battered British vehicles also traveled down the road lined with blackened, leafless trees, attempting to get back to the area that was held by the British. The Allied vehicles drove over the dead bodies of British and German infantry spread-eagle across the road. It was impossible to stop and move each body off of the road due to the sporadic gunfire and shelling from both sides of the battle. Kristian's nightmare was not over; the 12th SS Panzer counter-attacked and German tanks suddenly crashed through the trees almost on top of a staging area where the British gathered their wounded to ready them for transport back behind enemy lines.

Kristian watched the carnage and heard the wounded men's screams as they were crushed beneath the tracks of the advancing Panzer tanks. "Oh lord," Kristian said out loud to himself, wanting to look away, but not able to as the morbid event unfolded. "What a hell of a way to go." One of the Panzers exploded in a ball of fire without warning as a mortar bomb landed directly in its open turret. Two of the crew, screaming and on fire, escaped the burning tank but quickly fell to the ground, their burning bodies succumbing to the flame. One of the Panzer's guns received a direct hit from an 88mm shell and the tank's turret jammed from the explosion.

The crew bailed out, expecting it to blow at any moment, but only the tank commander, an NCO, and the radioman were able to leap down and escape alive. When the tank failed to explode, they remounted, with the exception of the tank's radio operator, who refused to leave the ditch along the road that he had taken refuge in. It became clear that the attack had failed; the two surviving tanks withdrew. Kristian stayed hidden at the edge of the cornfield until the area was clear of enemy soldiers, then began his escape once again. Kristian walked over to the tank whose turret had received a direct hit, strangely curious and wanting to see what happens inside of a tank when exposed to a direct hit

The explosion of a mortar in the confined space of the tank had devastated everything inside and caused the ammo for the tank's cannon and .50 caliber machine-gun to go up as well. On the floor of the turret was what was left of the crew. They were burnt to a cinder, teeth bared in a twisted macabre smile. Kristian had seen men who had been killed this way before and had been assigned to remove the bodies of the men who had been killed inside these vehicles. In some cases, they had to use a shovel to get them off the floor, their bodies fused from the intense heat.

Kristian crawled down from the tank and headed toward the safety of Falaise, knowing that it was still held by German troops. As Kristian crossed a creek he noticed the body of a dead SS soldier lying along the creek bed. The back of his head looking vaguely familiar as he walked over to take a closer look. Kristian rolled the body over to see the soldier's face. It was Philip, one of the boys from Kristian's platoon that was also trying to escape from the deadly British advance. Philip's wife had presented him with a baby boy a few weeks before D-Day, and he was very proud to have had a son. Since the day Philip had found out that he was a father, he carried a pair of little baby blue booties in his shirt pocket. He said that his son would always be close to his heart.

Kristian began to tear up thinking about the loss of Philip and the fact that the son he never had the chance to see would grow up fatherless, not even knowing who he was. Kristian began to chuckle thinking about the time he, Philip and a few other boys had got drunk on wine that they had liberated a French cellar. Philip had drunk too much and began to get sick that evening on the way back to their billets. As the group of inebriated boys passed by the commandant's command vehicle, Philip stopped and braced himself from falling to the ground on the vehicle's car door. Philip stood there for a moment as if to get his composure then suddenly stuck his head inside of the vehicle and threw up all over the commander's front seat. All of the boys stood there in disbelief for a moment, surprised at what they had just seen, then erupted in loud uncontrollable laughter.

The boys quickly grabbed Philip and took him back to the billets before they were discovered. Hell would have surely rained down upon them had they been caught by an officer. Kristian looked into Philip's face one last time with a loving smile then closed his eyes and said a quick prayer for his fallen comrade. "I'll never forget you, my friend," he said as he patted

328

Philip in his chest, then Kristian stood up and continued on to Falaise. On the outskirts of Falaise, Kristian stopped in a wooded area to make sure he didn't see any Allied troops before entering the town. Seeing that there was no immediate danger, Kristian continued his way into town, keeping an eye out for any enemy activity. As Kristian reached the town, he spotted a group of armed partisans standing in the road talking, about a block down the street.

Kristian had to cross the road the partisans were standing on to reach the safety and concealment of the buildings on the edge of town. He knew he had to make it to the safety of the buildings before being spotted by the partisans or he was a dead man. The partisans did not take any SS prisoners; they were usually shot immediately where they stood. At the first opportunity Kristian thought he could make it across the road without being spotted, he sprinted across the road to the sanctuary of the buildings on the other side. Before he had made it completely across the road, one of the partisans caught him out of the corner of his eye and alerted the others that he had seen a German soldier running across the road and into town.

The partisans gave chase after Kristian and he quickly ran into one of the vacated buildings to hide from them and certain death. He peered out of one of the windows facing the street and could see the partisans splitting up, searching each of the buildings one by one. Kristian moved away from the window in search of a place to hide from the partisan's that would surely come into the building looking for him. He dashed behind a stack of boxes as one of the partisans opened the door of the building and walked inside in search of his prey. Kristian hid quietly behind the boxes to avoid capture, but it was to no avail, the trail of mud from Kristian's boots led the partisan directly to him. Kristian felt the dangerous end of a rifle barrel poking into his back, then dropped his head and let out a sigh of dread, reluctantly accepting that the war and his life was now over.

"Get up," the partisan ordered Kristian with a poke of his rifle into Kristian's back. Kristian raised his hands and slowly stood up, then turned to face the man who was about to take his life. Both the partisan and Kristian looked at each other wide eyed in disbelief. It was Henry, Holly's cousin whose life he had once saved from certain death. "Henry," Kristian said with a smile of relief. "I can't believe it's you."

Henry stood there looking at Kristian with a hateful stone-faced look. "You once saved my life, so I owe you one," Henry said reluctantly.

"Go out the back door; no one is back there and you can slip away."

A wonderful feeling of relief came over Kristian. "Thank you, Henry," Kristian told him with a smile, then began to walk to the back door to make his escape but, was stopped by Henry blocking his way with his rifle.

"I owe you nothing now," Henry said, still as stone-faced as before, then poked Kristian towards the door.

Kristian carefully made his way through the town so as not to be discovered by any more partisans or Allied troops, then stumbled into a German patrol making its way through the rubble covered streets.

"Hey Kristian," one of the men in the patrol shouted. It was Gunny, Karl and Art, all with big greeting smiles relieved to see Kristian still alive. The sound of Allied Sherman tanks headed their way came from down the street and the boys quickly ran for cover. All of the men prepared themselves and readied their weapons for the bloody battle that was about to take place. Gunny prepped the Panzerfaust anti-tank weapon he had been carrying and waited for the tank to come into range, determined to take it out.

Chapter Thirty

Gunny stood up and pointed the Panzerfaust at the British manned Sherman tank. "Get down," Kristian yelled at Gunny. "You're going to get yourself killed you idiot." But before Gunny could fire the Panzerfaust, a 50 caliber round fired from the turret of the Sherman tank and blew off Gunny's lower jaw. Gunny dropped the Panzerfaust to the ground and began frantically trying feel his face for his missing jaw. Both Kristian and Gunny looked at each other in disbelief, their eyes wide open in shock at the horror they were experiencing. Gunny held out his blood-covered hand to Kristian. His arm stretched out as if trying to reach for Kristian while creating a panicked gurgling, groaning sound from his throat, unable to form words from the missing lower half of his face.

As young Gunny slowly stepped toward Kristian struggling to reach him, Gunny's head exploded throwing blood, flesh and bone in every direction. He had been hit from another round of the British 50 caliber machine-gun. The young man's body fell to the ground like a domino that was being pushed over on to its side. Kristian laid there behind the safety of the rubble staring at Gunny's lifeless body, confused and trying to comprehend how this could be when moments before they were both sharing a cigarette, laughing and joking around. Fear and a shiver ran down Kristian's spine as he suddenly contemplated his own mortality. Would this be his destiny as well, Kristian thought to himself?

Karl looked at Art, the boy shaking in fear of what hell was coming for them. "We are going to be fine," Karl told Art as Karl patted Art's leg in reassurance. "Get ready to charge," Karl said as he looked at the oncoming enemy peeking over the top edge of the bomb crater that they had been sheltering themselves in from enemy fire. Karl looked down at Art to make sure that he was readying himself for the assault and, as he looked down, Karl saw Art point his pistol under his chin and fire his weapon. The round from the pistol went through his head and exploded out of the top of Art's helmet, spraying his blood in a thick mist all over Karl's face.

Karl stood there with a horrified and disbelieving stare at what he had just seen his buddy do. A rifle round fired from an advancing enemy soldier hit the top of Karl's helmet, jerking his head back. The round did no harm to Karl but it brought him out of the trance his buddy's unbelievable and unexpected death had put him into. An uncontrollable rage and anger came over Karl, gnashing his teeth as if trying to hold himself together in an attempt not to explode.

Karl screamed with determined rage to get some sort of vengeance for his buddy's death as he climbed his way out of the bomb crater. Karl readied his rifle as if to thrust his bayonet into an enemy's chest and ran towards the Allied lines screaming like a mad man. An Allied soldier manning a 50-caliber machine-gun atop a Sherman tank took aim at Karl and gave a quick burst of fire, the rounds sliced through Karl's body ripping him in half.

Karl's upper torso fell to the rubble covered road, his eyes wide open in shock and gasping for air as his legs continued running two more steps before tumbling over and falling to the ground. With nothing he could do to help and it being impossible to hold off the Allied advance, Kristian decided it was time to find Holly and escape to German held territory.

Kristian ran into Holly's house, desperately trying to find her. The British were just a few hundred meters away from her house fighting hand to hand from house to house and room to room against the German SS units. Kristian had to find her and get her out of there quick before the British reached her home. Kristian searched the house but could not find her. Just before he left the house he heard the muffled sounds of a woman talking upstairs, and quickly ran up the stairs hoping to find Holly. Kristian opened the door to the room from where he had heard the woman's voice, and when he entered the room his eyes grew wide in disbelief at what he was seeing. It was Holly. But she was on a radio talking with the British giving them the location of the German troops. "Holly," Kristian said in disbelief. "What are you doing?" Holly dropped the microphone to the radio and quickly grabbed a pistol and pointed it at Kristian.

"Don't come any closer," Holly ordered him, reluctantly willing to sacrifice the man she loved for the liberation of her country. "I'll shoot you. Leave, get out of here while you still have a chance."

"It was you," Kristian said, finally figuring out how the partisans and the British seemed to know their every move. "You're part of the resistance. Everything I told you, you relayed to the enemy and gave us away. That's why you were at the British air drops and how the resistance got the information about our unit coming on the train to Normandy. You're a traitor."

"No Kristian," Holly said. "I'm a patriot. I'm a Frenchwoman, and the Germans are our enemy. They invaded my home and killed my people and now it is time for retribution."

"Holly," Kristian said aching in his heart. "I love you, I thought you loved me. Was it all a lie?"

"No Kristian," Holly said. "I love you more than life itself. That's why I'm not going to shoot. Leave while you can. The British are almost here; please go, save yourself,"

"No Holly," Kristian pleaded. "I won't leave here without you. I won't tell anyone, I swear and we can still have a wonderful life together,"

"Kristian," Holly said. "I love you, but it's over. Go, before it's too late. If not for you, then for me."

From outside, on the road in front of the house, Kristian and Holly heard men yelling at each other in English. Kristian knew now that he had to leave or risk capture or death. Kristian looked at Holly one last time with loving eyes, "I love you, Holly; never forget that." Kristian reluctantly but quickly turned and ran back down the stairs in an attempt to make an escape. Once downstairs Kristian peeked out of the front door to see if the coast was clear and seeing no one, Kristian slowly walked out. About two meters outside the door, a British patrol walking his direction from the left spotted him. At the same time, a German patrol was coming from the right direction. When the

British and Germans spotted Kristian they also spotted each other, then all hell broke loose.

Both patrols opened fire on each other with machine-gun and rifle fire, then began to hurl grenades at each other. Kristian, being in a very deadly situation standing in the middle of this frantic fire fight, dove back into Holly's house in an effort to avoid the carnage that was taking place outside her front door. A rifle round went through the helmet and into the brain of an SS man, killing him instantly, and two British soldiers were strafed across their chests with machine-gun fire, killing them. Both enemies continued killing each other off one by one until there were only two British soldiers and five SS men left still alive. The two British soldiers decided to call off the fight and tried to quickly escape from the Germans and make it back to British-held territory. Just as they both stood to run, a grenade thrown by one of the SS troops exploded, killing them both.

Kristian and Holly looked at each other with sorrow in their eyes, both knowing that soon, they would have to part. Kristian had to escape from the village to keep from becoming a prisoner of the British. He knew that he would be imprisoned until the war was over, or shot on site for being SS. On the other hand, Holly had no desire to surrender. If captured by the Germans, she would be tortured and raped until she finally succumbs to death. But Holly knew that she had to stay to inform the British what she knew about German troop movements, in an effort to help win the war and liberate her beloved country.

Kristian softly kissed Holly goodbye, reluctantly having to leave to avoid capture. Kristian began to walk to the door to make his escape, then suddenly turned around. Kristian looked deep and lovingly into her eyes. "I can't leave you Holly." Holly, relieved in her heart, ran to Kristian. She embraced him, burying her head deep into his chest. "I won't let them take you Holly." Kristian said, as he wrapped his strong loving arms around her. "All we can do now is pray." Holly said, as if peacefully accepting their fate.

As they held each other, they heard heavy footsteps coming up the stairs. They did not know if they were British or German troops, but they did know that one of their lives, was truly in peril. The footsteps drew closer and closer, their hearts

340

were pounding in fear; then suddenly the footsteps stopped.

Kristian and Holly looked at each other, as if confused to why

they no longer heard them. With a loud crash, the soldiers kicked

in the door. Both Kristian, and Holly, jumped in shock and fear

seeing two soldiers pointing rifles at them, fixed with razor sharp

bayonets. "Get your bloody hands in the air, you damn dirty

kraut," one of the soldiers ordered. To Holly's relief, the soldiers

were British. But she knew she must think of something fast, or

Kristian would surely spend years in a prisoner of war camp.

"Stop." Holly yelled at the British soldiers, as

she stood between them shielding Kristian. The two

soldiers stoped their advance toward Kristian and looked

at Holly, puzzled by her request. "He is one of us."

Holly shouted to the soldiers. The two British soldiers,

still confused, looked at each other then back at Holly.

"What do you mean he's one of us?" one of the British

soldiers said.

Holly thought to herself, "*what am I going to*

say?" then quickly had an idea of what to do. "I'm part

of the French resistance. I've been radioing England,

informing them on the Germans. He has been relaying me information on troop strength, and troop movements. He, is also a spy for the allies.

"Well chap, I guess you're a real hero then." One of the British soldiers said with a smile and a congratulatory pat on Kristian's back.

Kristian, not knowing English still had no idea what was going on and was standing there with a look of confusion on his face. "Do either of you speak German?" Holly asked the two soldiers.

"No mam." One of the soldiers replied.

"Okay, let me explain to him what's happening. He doesn't understand English, and you can see how confused he is about what is going on. He must be going crazy with curiosity." Both of the soldiers smiled and their nodded their head yes, then Holly began to explain to Kristian her idea to save him taken prisoner.

"I've a plan to keep you from a prison of war camp so, listen carefully." Holly told Kristian. "I told them you were a spy, relaying messages to me about the

342

Germans since we met. If you are questioned, tell them you're having memory problems due to the head wound you received in an air raid, and I'll fill you in the rest later."

With a cy of relief, Kristian looked at Holly smiled. "I love you Holly, always and forever," then tenderly kissed her lips. The two British soldiers looked at each other and smiled, seeing their youth and the love they have for each other.

"Okay you two," one of the British soldiers told them "Let's get you back to our lines before we get ourselves killed in here." Holly took Kristian's hand, and for a moment shared a smile, looking lovingly into each other's eyes. They would now be safe, and free from this horrible war. Then together, they followed the soldiers to the safety of allied held territory. For Kristian and Holly, the war was over. Now they can have a future and a family together, free from the nightmares of war.

After the war. Holly wrote a very successful novel about her part in the war effort in defeating the tyranny of the Nazi's, and the liberation of France.

Kristian and Holly spent the rest of their days together,

traveling the world with their three beautiful children.

Together, sharing a love that was tested like few others

ever have.

THE END